SHADE

ROYAL DEVILS GEORGIA

ERIN TREJO

CHAPTER ONE

SHADE

"How's it feel?" I ask my cousin, Bull, as he stands proudly wearing his cut. He's worked hard to get that patch, and tonight, we party with him.

"Feels fuckin' great, man. I don't even have words," he says as I slap a hand on his shoulder. I know how much that patch means to him. He's worked his ass off as a prospect in the background over the past year to earn it. I'm proud as fuck for all that he's accomplished.

"Looks fuckin' good on you, brother," Maverick declares as he walks up with beers in his hands, passing us each one. I take mine and down a long drink before raising it in a toast to Bull.

"To this asshole for finally makin' the cut. You worked hard over the past year, and that means a lot to us." We clink bottles before taking down the rest of the beer and cheering loudly. This is how we party when we patch in a new member. We party hard and let them know they are welcome and appreciated.

"Thanks, brother."

"FEELS WEIRD CALLIN' your cousin brother now, huh?" Mav asks him. Bull nods his head.

"A little, but we've always been pretty close. Probably more so than the rest of the family," Bull replies.

"He's right. This little fucker used to follow me around in his goddamn diaper. It's really good to have you here, a part of us," I tell him. He nods his thanks when Tyrant walks over.

"Havin' a good time?"

"Yeah. A damn good time," he answers. The music is blasting, and people are everywhere. Even a few out-of-town chapters are here celebrating with us. It's one good fucking time.

"There's plenty of pussy to go around tonight," Tyrant adds. I chuckle and glance around, noticing there are a lot more girls around tonight. That's a plus in my book. In fact, I grab the closest one I can find and yank her in front of me before nodding toward my cousin.

"Newly patched member. He needs the special treatment," I tell her. She licks her lips as she gazes at Bull, ready to please him in any way he tells her to. It's almost amusing to watch the way he smirks at her.

"Is that right? You're the newest?" she purrs as she steps in front of him, running her hand down his chest.

"That's right. You gonna make me happy?" he asks, causing us to chuckle. She's going to do more than that, I can tell by the look in her eyes. She's horny and ready to ride his ass already.

"I'm going to make you so happy," she coos as she grabs his hand and leads him away from the group. I laugh aloud as I watch the bastard walk away with her.

"Wasn't that nice? You got him a present," Mav says.

"I do try. I am the nice one of the group," I almost hold my grin back.

"Yeah, the nice one. You didn't seem so nice when you were blowin' that assholes head off earlier," he reminds me of the job we were on.

"Business. It was all business."

"Speakin' of business. We need to talk about that load we're followin' up to South Carolina. That route is hot," Tyrant adds. That doesn't sound good to me, but it is what it is. We still have to move the load, no matter how hot the area is.

"That gonna be an issue?"

"Might be. Those Irish fucks are out there lookin' to take our pipelines. They should know better, but just in case they don't, we might need a little extra manpower on that load." I nod my head. Nothing wrong with having extra manpower.

"I think that's smart. Add a few more guys. It won't hurt anything," Mav agrees.

"Probably will. We don't need to lose a load of guns to the Irish. That would start a war with the Russians, and we don't need that shit comin' our way."

"Heard that," I mumble.

"I'm thinkin' about lettin' Bull in on that run. You good with that?" Ty asks me. I nod my head.

"Why wouldn't I be? He's patched now."

"It could get dangerous, and it'll be his first run as a patched member," he reminds me.

"I know. He's got this. I think he can handle himself," I reassure them. Mav grunts his agreement as Ty nods his head.

"Just wanted to get your thoughts on it, is all."

"He's good. He's got this," I repeat.

"Then he's in. So are you," Ty tells me. I nod my head and motion to one of the girls for another beer.

She nods and strolls toward the bar as I watch her ass swishing back and forth. I'll be in that ass tonight. I can feel it.

"Stop starin' so hard," Ty laughs loudly.

"Can't help it. You saw that ass of hers," I tell him.

"She's pretty new around here. You sure you should corrupt her already?" Mav asks. I chuckle and rub the back of my neck.

"I wouldn't corrupt her. I would make her not want the rest of you assholes, is all."

"You can keep that. I don't need it," Mav tells us as I laugh.

"Yeah, your old lady would have your nuts if you touched that," I tell him. He nods his head, drinking his beer like he doesn't even notice the girl coming our way. It's a funny thing seeing the guys fall for only one woman.

"She would."

"Here you go," Amber, the new girl, says. I take my beer and grab her wrist with the other hand, dragging her against me.

"You wanna hang out with me tonight?" I ask, whispering in her ear. She looks up at me, licking her lips, and I know I've sealed the deal. She nods her head, a little shyness creeping through her façade. I lean down and press my lips to hers, kissing her until she's breathless. Then I pull away and smack her ass, watching her walk away with heated pink cheeks.

"You're gettin' that tonight," Ty says.

"Already knew that, brother. I already knew that."

CHAPTER TWO

AVERY

"Come on. Let's get you up," I tell Lance. He's paralyzed from the waist down, and it's time to move him from the bed to his chair. He hates this part because I do most of the lifting.

"Do you know how much I hate this?"

"Which part?"

"All of it. Having a girl lift me into a chair is embarrassing," he mumbles as I lift him and move him to the chair.

"I don't think it's that embarrassing."

"I do. Look at me," he snaps, pointing to himself. I see him. The real him. He's a great guy who typically has a great attitude toward life. Today must be a bad day for him.

"I see you, Lance," I tell him as I adjust his legs. He brushes my hands away and does it himself.

"What's with you today? You're not usually like this," I ask, needing to know where his head is.

"I'm just sick of everything today. Of you doing everything for me."

"It's kind of what I do," I tease him a little, but he doesn't smile. Instead, he sits there sulking. "You can't change it, Lance. It is what it is." He finally looks up at me and sighs.

"I know. I'm sorry. I don't make your job much easier on you, do I?"

"You know I don't mind your attitude. I get used to it," I reply truthfully. Unfortunately, Lance isn't the only patient I have who likes to get grouchy on me, and he won't be the last.

"You shouldn't have to. I shouldn't be such an ass," he speaks softly.

"I get it, you know. I might not be in your position, but I get it."

"It's hard some days. I just want to scream and shit, but there is nothing that will ever change this," he says, breaking my heart. I hate seeing people aren't coping well with the situation they are in. I hate seeing the depression in their eyes, the hopelessness. I hope I ease some of that by being here to help, but mostly, I feel like the burden. They don't like me coming around to remind them that they can't do things independently or stand and walk through the house. They hate that I can, and they resent that a lot of the time.

"I know this is hard, and you're new to this, but it gets better. It gets easier, and one day, you won't need me coming around to bug you," I tell him with a smile.

"You don't bug me, Avery. I just hate this is all."

"I know you do, but it'll get easier. I promise."

"I need to work on my muscles to be able to use my arms better."

"Then we work on that. Where are the weights?" I ask him. He points to the closet, and I walk over, pulling the door open. I grab the smallest weights off the floor and return, passing them to him. He starts to do his workout while I check a few things on my phone. I check for any new work-related emails but don't find any. Then I'm back by Lance's side, watching him as he works.

"I don't think it's going to take long for you to gain muscle," I encourage him. He's already pretty in shape. Well, before his accident, he was.

"Why is that?"

"You're in pretty good shape as it is," I tell him.

"Are you checking me out, Avery?" I giggle a little and shake my head.

"That would be against the rules."

"Fuck the rules. Go out with me tomorrow."

"Where do you want to go?"

"Dinner. You'll have to drive, though," he grins.

"I can do that. I could also get in trouble for this," I remind Lance.

"It's only dinner. We're practicing my skills in this chair," he quips, making me laugh.

"Okay. Deal. We'll go to dinner. But I expect you to be on your best behavior."

"When I have I ever not been?" he teases. I won't lie and say Lance isn't attractive because he is. He's also a great person.

"I haven't seen you being a shithead yet, but I have a feeling it's in there somewhere," I smile at him.

"You think I lost my skills in the accident?"

"Not a chance. You might have lost use of your legs, but I have a feeling you don't need them to charm the ladies anyway."

"THANKS, Avery. For everything. I mean it. I know I don't make things easier on you, but you always keep my ass in check."

"That's my job. Help you where I can and to slap your ass back into reality," I tease.

"Beautiful and funny. Great combo, Avery."

"I'll take that as a compliment."

"It is." His hand comes out to grab mine, and he tugs me toward him. I lean down just enough that he can kiss me if he wants to, and at first, I think Lance might, but then he pulls back.

"I'll save that for tomorrow."

"You have a game plan, do you?" I ask playfully.

"It involves my lips on yours," he says confidently.

"Is that a challenge?" I ask him. His lips are still a breath away, and I almost want to know what they feel like. I know it's all wrong since I'm supposed to be here helping him, not dating him. But what can it hurt? He's a good guy.

"Well, I think it's about time I get going. Your other nurse will be here in a few minutes to work with your legs," I tell him. He looks at me and drops his hand before I slowly pull away.

"I don't think you should flirt with her," I tell him with a giant smirk on my face.

"Why? You jealous?"

"No, she's sixty-five and married. I don't think she's your type," I laugh.

"She might be my type, Avery. You don't know what my type is."

"Well, in that case, enjoy your flirting." I wave at

him over my shoulder as I walk out of the room and meet Janice in the living room.

"He's all ready for you," I inform her with a smile.

CHAPTER THREE

SHADE

The bikes are lined up, ready to ride. The guys are on edge, knowing this could turn ugly at any second. I'm ready for it to get ugly. I'm in the mood for some bloody mayhem. It's been a while since we've had a good war around here, and I'd say it's needed to keep us on our game.

"What are you smilin' about?" Cowboy asks as he slides his gun into the back of his jeans.

"Nothin'. Just hopin' somethin' good pops off on this run."

"Are you shittin' me? You want a war?"

"Why not? We haven't had shit goin' on around here in a while. We might as well fuck up some Irish cunts," I tell him truthfully. I wouldn't mind going a few rounds with the Irish. They've been trying to get at us for a while now, and if they plan on fucking with us when we're on this run, it's the perfect time to fuck them back.

"You're sick, brother."

"I'm ready." That's a statement. I'm ready for whatever comes my way today. I check my guns and shove one into the back of my jeans, the other in the front. Whichever one I can grab first is the one I'll go with.

"Yo, Ty. This motherfucker is wantin' a war," Cowboy calls out to Tyrant. He strolls over with a grin on his face.

"He wouldn't be alone then. I'm about ready to get dirty too." Just as he finishes speaking, his phone rings. Ty pulls it out and answers it, his face immediately falling at whatever's being said. I shift from foot to foot, waiting for him to get off and tell us what's happening. A few 'yeah's' later, and he's hanging up.

"A chapter up north just got the shit beat out of them," he says.

"What do you mean?"

"They were attacked. Guess who attacked them?" he asks, a sick grin crossing his face.

"The fuckin' Irish?" I ask, more than ready to get my hands dirty now.

"Yeah. No good motherfuckers beat the hell out of them. Sent two to the hospital," he adds. Fuck. That isn't good.

"They all good?"

"They will be. Just keep your fuckin' eyes open on this run. They're out there," he warns before turning to address the whole room. He repeats the information and the warning, and the room erupts in roars and chaos. I figured it would.

"Told you it was time for a war," I say, turning to Cowboy. He nods his head as we filter out the door and climb on our bikes. The shipment is here, ready to be loaded into the back of the van.

"I mean it, keep your eyes open," Ty says once more. I nod my head as the others do the same. Then we're taking off out of the parking lot and following the van. A few guys are out front, keeping watch a few miles ahead of us. We don't want any surprises, but I'd sure as hell take one. My finger itches to get on that trigger.

The ride is going to take a while, and I'm glad about that. It's been too long since I've been out on the open road like this. The wind whips past me, the rumble of my bike beneath me. This is what freedom feels like. This is what it feels like to fucking fly. You can be yourself out here, and no one cares. Just sit quietly and not say a word and still feel everything. It's not something everyone gets a chance in life to experience, that's for sure.

The ride is going smoothly, which kind of pisses me off. I was ready for a showdown.

Then a tire on the van blows, and it swerves to the side of the road. I pull out my cell and call ahead, letting them know we're stopping. The rest of us pull over as the man driving climbs out. One shot is all it takes for him to go down. The rest of us pull our guns and begin scanning the area, trying to locate where that shot came from. That's when I see the guys coming back. Fuck they're right in the line of fire.

Cowboy waves his hands in the air, telling them to go back, but it's too late. More shots are fired, and we fire back. Then I see Bull's bike hit, and he begins to lose control. The bike skids across the pavement, flipping and throwing Bull into the rocks that line the road.

"Fuck!" I roar as I try and race toward him. I call his name, hoping like hell that someone's covering my ass as I go. More shots are fired until everything slowly dies down.

"Bull?" I call his name as I kneel next to him.

"Fuck me," he grumbles.

"You're hurt. Where?"

"I can't feel shit, Shade. I don't feel shit," he tells me. That immediately sets off warning bells in my head. Something is wrong. This isn't right. He can't feel anything. I search his body for bullet holes or anything like that, but I don't find any.

"You're gonna be okay," I tell him, praying to God that it isn't a lie.

"I can't feel shit," he grumbles once more.

"What the hell happened?" Ty asks when he comes over and takes a look at him.

"Shot his bike. He was thrown. Get the van out of here, and I'll deal with the cops. He needs an ambulance," I tell him as I pull out my phone and dial.

"Fuck!" Ty yells. "I knew this was comin'."

"You didn't know they'd be waitin'. Get the van out of here!" I tell him one more time. He nods his head, slapping a hand on my shoulder before I hear him hollering to the others. The bikes rev and take off along with the van as I listen for the sounds of sirens to come our way.

"Am I dyin'?" Bull asks me.

"Hell no. You just got patched in, you fucker."

"I can't feel my legs, Shade."

"It's just from bein' thrown. You'll be okay."

"What if I'm not?"

"You are. Shut the fuck up bein' a downer, man. You just got your patch and already actin' like a bitch," I chuckle, although I'm worried as hell about him not feeling anything.

"You're a bitch," he grins up at me. I hear the sirens in the distance, and finally, they arrive.

They load Bull up on a stretcher and put him in the back of the ambulance as the cop questions me. I make up some shit about him hitting a rock and flying off the road until Ty can get with the Chief and pay this shit off. They don't question me for long before sending me on my way.

I'm allowed to follow the ambulance to the hospital, and I can only imagine that's because Ty made the right calls. You don't see a bunch of shell casings and send someone on their way.

Nevertheless, I followed behind them, and now I'm in the waiting room waiting to hear anything about how he's doing.

My nerves are firing off. It's been hours. The guys are on their way back after dropping the load off without any extra drama.

Ty's the first to walk in, followed by Mav and Cowboy.

"Where's the rest?" I ask.

"Sent them back to the clubhouse. Didn't figure he'd need an audience just yet," Ty answers. I nod my head and rest it in my hands.

"Haven't heard anything?"

"No. Not a damn thing." It's been hours. What the hell could take hours?

I shift in my chair, not liking this at all. I need to know that my cousin is alive and well. Shit, he just patched in, and now he's lying in a bed in this place.

After another two hours, the doctor finally came out and talked to us. It isn't what I thought I'd hear either.

"He's paralyzed from the waist down," he announces as the world shifts and spins around me. No fucking way. He can't be. There's no way he can be.

"I'm sorry," he says as I lunge at him. Tyrant grabs ahold of me and pulls me back as I scream.

"He can't fuckin' be paralyzed! He can't be!"

"Calm down, Shade," he warns me. I take a few deep breaths before I compose myself. They said we could go back and see him, but what the hell do I say? How do I look at him and not break down? All he's ever wanted was to be a part of this club, and now he can't ever ride again. His first goddamn run and this is what happens to him? It's fucked up. It's wrong, and it's my fault. I shouldn't have let him on this run. I should have told Ty no when he asked. What the fuck is wrong with me? Why didn't I say no?

"Get the fuck out of your head, Shade. He needs his brothers now. Not your fuckin' sulkin' bullshit."

"Fuck you! I said to send him on that ride," I

growl at Tyrant. He sees the anger, the rage in my eyes, and he welcomes that shit with open arms. When I lunge at him, he's ready. He slams his fist into my face moments before mine impacts with his. I take out my rage on him when it isn't his fault. He hits me a few good times, and then we're being pulled apart by the guys.

"You put him on this run!"

"Blame me, Shade, but that doesn't change the facts. He's still lyin' in there waitin' on us. On you!" He roars as I wipe the blood from my lip. I know my eye is already turning black, but I don't care. Instead, I turn and storm down the hall in the direction that doctor told us Bull was. I find his room and walk inside, not ready for this.

"What the fuck happened to your face?" he asks when I walk closer to his bed.

"Had a little disagreement with Ty."

"Little my ass. He handed you your ass on a platter, brother."

"How you feelin'?"

"Doc told you the news, I'm sure. Don't make me repeat it."

"I fucked up. I shouldn't have let you gone on that run," I tell him.

"Like you could have stopped me. Fuck that. And besides, I'll get the feelin' back in my legs. I know I will. Doc said there's a lot of swellin' goin' on right now."

I ran my hand through my hair because I heard what he said. He's never going to walk again. There is no coming back from this.

"You sound confident," I tell him.

"I am. I just got my goddamn patch, Shade. Don't count me out yet," he says, breaking my fucking heart in half.

"Heard that," I say, playing the part. Who the hell am I to set his dreams on fire?

"The guys here?"

"Ty, Mav, and Cowboy are. The others went back to the clubhouse for now," I tell him as he nods his head. He raises his hand and scratches at his jaw.

"Could have been worse, yeah?" I don't know how he figures that. I would be dead if I couldn't ride. That's the only way.

"Guess so. You could have been in a body bag," I tell Bull, causing him to laugh.

"Don't sugar coat it," he adds.

"Wouldn't dream of it."

"I'm glad you're here."

"Me too, brother. Just sorry this shit happened to you."

"Stop all the girly bullshit. No one wants to hear that shit," Tyrant declares as he strolls into the room.

"I tried to tell him," Bull adds, nodding toward me.

"Heard that. How you feelin'?"

"Like I was hit by a fuckin' truck. You sure the van didn't run my ass over?" Bull asks with a laugh.

"Pretty damn sure. You flew through the fuckin' air, though, brother."

"Doc said there's no fixin' my back." Now I can hear the sadness in his tone. I can hear the regret and the anger.

"We don't know that. Hell, you might be a goddamn walkin' miracle when this is over," Tyrant says, causing us all to chuckle.

"Might be. But if I'm not, are you strippin' my colors?" There it is. The one question that would linger in my mind too. The one that's a make it or break it question.

"No. You just got those motherfuckers. You got a long time of bein' in this club, asshole." I release a breath of relief for him. Some clubs would strip his colors for being in a wheelchair, and Tyrant has every right to do that. He's the Prez, and he makes that call.

"Thanks, brother. I don't think I could handle this shit without you guys."

"You don't have to. We got you, brother."

CHAPTER FOUR

AVERY

I'm hesitant as I walk to the door of the clubhouse where my patient is staying. I've never been to an MC clubhouse before. This is all new to me, and I don't know what to expect.

I raise my hand and knock, but after a few tries with no one answering, I pull on the handle, and it opens. I step inside and hear music playing and figure that's why they didn't hear me.

"Hello?" I call out when I don't see anyone. A second later, a man walks out of one of the side rooms and comes toward me.

"Who are you?"

"I'm Avery. I'm Daniel's nurse," I tell him. He eyes me up and down before he nods his head and motions for me to follow him. We walk through the room before he stops and turns to face me.

"He's been havin' a tough time adjustin'. He thinks he's gonna get better," the guy tells me. I nod my head. Most of my patients do think they'll get better, and there's nothing wrong with thinking that. Some do, and others just learn to live with it.

"I'll talk with him."

"No, you won't. You're not here to talk to him. You're here to help him," he snaps, sounding pissed that I'd even attempt to talk to the man.

"My job is to help him overcome the obstacles he's going to face. He needs to know that this is permanent."

"I said you aren't tellin' him that. You can either take it or leave it, sweetheart, and at this point, I'm debatin' about askin' for a new nurse." The growl that leaves his throat is a little menacing. I nod my head quickly, understanding what he's saying perfectly. I've never been fired from a job, and I don't plan to be today.

"I understand."

"Good. Follow me," he says. I follow him down the hall and into a room that I assume they use for working out. There are machines all over, but I notice the bed in the corner. This must be where my patient is staying.

"Is this his room?" I ask, glancing around when I

see him at the far side of the room. He faces the wall, his head down.

"Yeah, for now. He didn't want to be carried up and down the steps," the guy tells me.

"Yo, Bull. Your nurse is here," he calls out. Slowly the man's head rises, and I see his shoulders rise and fall before he turns his chair to face us with a smile plastered across his face. I know that's just for show.

"Hey. I'm Bull," he greets me as he rolls toward us.

"Bull, huh? Thought it was Daniel?" I tease a little.

"I go by Bull."

"Bull it is. I'm Avery," I extend my hand toward him. Just like most of my polite patients, he offers his hand in return. He shakes mine before pulling away.

"I think I can handle Avery, Shade. You don't need to stay," he tells the guy that's hovering over us.

"Fine," he grunts and turns to walk away.

"He's intense," I say.

"My cousin. He's just worried about me, is all."

"Does he have a reason to be?" Bull looks up at me, shaking his head.

"I'm not gonna off myself if that's what you're askin' me."

"That's good to know. I don't like finding my patients dead," I admit to him.

"You've found them dead before?" he asks.

"Twice. It kills me each time too. There is so much life left to live, and I'm here to help you with that. I understand the feelings you have, and I want to help."

"You do, huh? You been paralyzed before?"

"I actually have when I was a kid. I fell off a swing that was pretty high up. It was only temporary, but I felt it. All the anger, rage, helplessness. I hated it."

"So you decided to help others?" he asks. That's when I noticed Shade, as he called him, sitting on a piece of equipment listening in. "Don't mind him. Overprotective motherfucker." I giggle.

"Yes, I decided I wanted to help others that were dealing with the same thing I had. Some get out of the chairs, others don't, but there is still so much to do."

"You don't think I'm gettin' out of this chair, do you?"

"I don't know all of your injuries."

"First off, don't lie to me, Avery. That will get you a long way with me." My eyes slowly slip over to Shade's before coming back to Bull's.

"Good. I won't sugarcoat shit for you. That's not

the kind of person I am. You're never walking again. I'm here to help you adjust to that and learn to do things on your own," I reply truthfully. I feel like Bull is one of those people who need it straight, and despite what Shade said, I will give it to him.

"What the hell did I say to you?" Shade is on his feet coming toward me when Bull rolls in between us.

"I want the truth. Not your half-ass shit, Shade. She's here for me, not you! So back the fuck off!" There's the anger I knew was lurking in there.

"She doesn't need to tell you shit that isn't true. The doc said," Shade begins, but Bull cuts him off.

"The doc said it's doubtful with my injuries. Just let it the fuck go, Shade. Let it go." Shade rubs at the back of his neck as if he's torn on what to do. Then he finally nods his head and storms out of the room, leaving Bull and me.

"Sorry about that," he says.

"Not the first time that's happened. A lot of people have faith, and I don't have a problem with that. They believe what they believe, and I know what I know."

"And you know as well as I do that I'm not leavin' this chair," he states. I nod my head as he sighs.

"You can still live a long, happy life. That's what

I'm here for. We'll work the muscles in your legs. We'll work the muscles in your arms. I'll teach you how to move around on your own."

"I won't need them hoverin' over me?" he asks. I shake my head.

"Thank fuck for that. They can be suffocatin' at times."

"I bet so. I know my mom was the same way. I had to figure things out on my own. I didn't like having everything done for me."

"You were younger, though. You didn't have the same kind of pride as an adult," he reminds me.

"That's true too. Okay, first things first. I want to teach you how to get in and out of bed on your own."

"Won't that be a fuckin' miracle."

"You can do it. You're a strong man. Come on." He wheels over behind me as I walk toward his bed in the corner. I look it over, and I'm actually glad they had a hospital bed brought in. That will make it a little easier on him.

"This is a good bed to start with," I tell him. We go over, lowering and raising the bed, so it's at his level before I teach him how to get in and out. He does it a few times on his own, and he seems proud of himself. Then we work his legs a little, and he works his arms. It makes me happy he's following my directions so easily.

"Good. I think you'll be fine. You're going to do great at therapy."

"Thanks, Avery. I appreciate all of this." I nod my head thinking all this is going to be easier than I thought it would. But people like him can be deceiving. I'll be talking with Shade before I leave here today.

"Well, I think we have it all covered for today," I tell him.

"Leavin' so soon?"

"I have other patients. I'll be back tomorrow," I tell him.

"How many days a week can I expect you?"

"Seven. You get me every day of the week. Isn't that great?" He looks up at me and flashes a sweet smile that I know is just for my benefit.

"Great. I can't wait."

"I bet. I'll see you tomorrow," I tell him before walking out of the room. When I step out, I see a bunch of men hanging around. I stop one and ask about Shade.

"Excuse me. Do you know where Shade is?"

"Damn, is he hittin' a doc now?" the man asks with a laugh.

"I'm Bull's nurse. Can I talk to you about him?"

"Nah, you better talk to Shade. That's his cousin," the guy tells me. "Come on," he says, and I follow behind him. That's when I spot Shade. He's standing at a bar with a drink in hand.

"This girl needs you, Shade," the guy tells him. Shade turns around his attention now on me. It makes me squirm a little that he's staring me down the way he is. He's intimidating.

"What?"

"He acts like he's the happiest man on the earth, but I know that's a lie. I need to know how he's doing when I'm not around."

"He's great," Shade says stiffly.

"Is he? He looked depressed when I first walked in. That can quickly get out of control," I tell him.

"And that means what? He isn't depressed. He has all of us on his side. You just do what you're supposed to do, and we'll handle the rest, sweetheart." I want to huff out a breath and argue, but there's no point. I've met men like Shade who don't think depression is a thing or that no one they care about could be affected by it. They're morons, if you ask me.

"Fine. I like to keep up with what's going on, good or bad, while I'm not here. Is that okay with you?" I ask in a snarky tone.

"That's fine, but there isn't much goin' on. Bull might get his cock sucked every once in a while, and he may eat a little pussy, but that's about it. He isn't in any shape to ride just yet."

"He isn't riding ever again, Shade." That's a fact. One he needs to come to terms with. He sets his drink in the bar next to him before stepping closer to me.

"You come here, do your job, and leave. You don't see the look in his eyes like we do, like I do. He can overcome anything. He can do this too."

"Has the doctor gone over his injuries with you?" I ask.

"Fuck the doctor. Fuck what they think and fuck you. No one needs your bullshit here, Avery. No one. Now, if you can't handle doin', what we're payin' you good money to do, then tell me now. I was told you were the best, but I'm debatin' that decision as we speak," Shade states, breaking me in half. How dare he? How dare he say that to me. Although I've been in this position before, I've never had a man speak to me this way.

"I can handle my job just fine. Be a good cousin and see if you can handle yours," I snap at him before brushing past and heading for the door. I've had enough for one day.

CHAPTER FIVE

"They're gonna pay for what they caused," I tell Ty as we sit around the table. There's no way I can let this shit slide, not now, not after what they did to Bull.

"They are," Ty agrees, and I'm thankful as fuck for that. I want revenge. I want to show Bull that this isn't all for nothing. I will make it right one asshole at a time if I have to.

"But we take our time," Maverick says, pissing me off more than I already am.

"What the hell does that mean?"

"It means just what I said. We take our time. We're not up against a small MC here, Shade. We're up against the fuckin' mafia. We have to play our cards right. They already got to the northern chapter. You want to end up like that?" he's right. One of the northern chapter guys lost an arm, the other an eye. I don't want anyone else from our chapter to get hurt.

"Fuck. Do you know how hard it is to wait this out when my cousin is in a goddamn chair?" I ask, looking around the room.

"He's our brother too, Shade. We're all pissed," he says. I nod my head. I know they are. I know they all like Bull too.

"It's just fucked. I had to tell his mom. My fuckin' aunt looks at me like I did this shit to him," I admit. The day I told her, she lost it. She came at me full force, and I let her pound on me until she couldn't hold herself up anymore. Then I held her. I fucking held my aunt in my arms while she fell apart. Bull refuses to see her right now. He said it's too soon, and he needs some time, and I don't push him. It's his life. She knows, and when he's ready, he will see her.

"You didn't do this. Bull put that cut on that mornin' just like the rest of us knowin' what could happen. He took that run the same way. None of us could have seen that comin'," Maverick says. I nod my head, knowing all this, but it still stings. It still fucking hurts that it had to be him. Not that I'd wish this on any of my brothers, I wouldn't but fuck, my own cousin.

"First things first. The strip club is under renovations. We're gonna lose money right there until we get it back up and runnin'. That shithole was just that. Once it's good to go, we move on to the shop. It could use an update too. As far as the Irish go, we start small. We work our way to the top." Tyrant gives us his plan.

"What do you mean small?" Cowboy asks.

"Just what I said. We start small. Street level. We fuck up a few things here and there. Nothin' that can be pointed at us. We work our way up the chain until we get where we want to be."

"I want whoever ordered that hit," I tell him.

"Which is at the top," Ty says. "We're not in any shape to go straight to the top. We need more men, more time, a plan. We start small." Everyone grunts their agreement, although I'd prefer to storm the motherfucker's mansion. I wouldn't care if I died in the act as long as he went to hell with me.

"When do we start?" I ask, ready to handle this shit.

"We make a plan, Shade. We don't just jump and start firin'."

"I know. So let's make a goddamn plan then."

"Street level. We hit their dealers. Let that part of their operation take a hit. Then we move up to the suppliers." Everyone nods, grunts, and agrees. I don't like this idea, but it is what it is. I have to follow whatever orders Ty sets in place for me.

"Fine. Let's do this shit," I say. Ty nods and slams down the gavel. I shove out of my chair and walk out the door, heading straight for the bar.

"Why are you always at the bar?" I look over at Bull as he rolls toward me.

"I like to drink."

"You're on edge," he says.

"So? Still like to drink," I tell him once more.

"You can't fix me, Shade. She can't either, no matter what she thinks," he tells me. I nod my head, knowing exactly who it is he's talking about. That damn nurse of his, Avery. She's so happy go lucky and thinks she can make the world a better place. Not our world she can't.

"She's good though, yeah?"

"Yeah. And sexy as fuck," he adds, causing me to chuckle.

"You would notice that," I say.

"How wouldn't I? Any straight man would."

"What are you two talkin' about?"

"The sexy nurse Shade set me up with. I made her show me how to do the weights a few times just so I could watch her ass when she'd bend over," Bull explains, making Cowboy laugh.

"No shit?"

"No shit. It was sweet," Bull adds.

"She isn't here for that," I remind him.

"She's here to help me, and by bendin' that sweet ass over, she helped a lot." His laughter is something I've missed since he's been in that chair. It hasn't been long, but still.

"You sure are happy today."

"Did you not see her, Shade? Any man would be happy to see that ass comin' his way," Bull tells me. I shake my head. That man is a mess.

"You thinkin' with your cock?"

"It doesn't work. I'm not thinkin' at all anymore," he laughs, though I can I hear the hurt in it. He isn't happy about this. Bull isn't okay with all this. He's just dealing with it, and I know that. I wish there were something more I could do. Something I could say to him, but there isn't, and there never will be. Instead, I bring my beer to my lips and take a long pull. I can't look at him and not feel guilty about all of this. I can't look him in the eyes and know that I caused this.

"You done yet?" I ask.

"What the fuck is your problem? I gotta deal with shit somehow," he adds. I know he does but with humor? Laughing like he's okay with all this? I know he isn't because I wouldn't be. I'm not.

I walk away and head for my room before pulling

out my cell phone and dialing her. I shouldn't be, but what the fuck do I do?

"Hello?"

"Avery? It's Shade."

"Is Bull okay?"

"He's fine. I just needed to ask you a question."

"Sure. What is it?"

"How do I look at him and not feel guilty for this?"

"I heard it was an accident," she murmurs into the line. Fuck. How do I tell her it wasn't? How do I tell her I sent him on that run? Fuck me.

"It's complicated." I pinch the bridge of my nose between my thumb and forefinger.

"It's not easy, Shade. But it's possible. He needs you now. He needs you to be strong when he can't. I see the way he is. Bull puts up a front, and I think it's all for you guys. He doesn't want you feeling bad about what happened, so he will put on that mask of happiness and humor and deal with it. You have to be stronger than that. You have to look past that façade and see what's really happening with him."

"He won't let me."

"It isn't about giving him a choice. It's about helping him. He needs you now. Bull needs that strength whether he wants to admit that or not. Just don't push him too hard."

"Fuck. I'll try. I don't know what the hell I'm doing," I admit.

"You're being a good cousin is what you're doing. He needs that now."

"Right. Thanks. Sorry I called you so late," I add.

"Feel free to call anytime. Day or night. I'm always here." With that, I hang up and run my hand through my hair. I feel like I'm somehow failing him by not going after these motherfuckers. I feel like I'm on the losing end with him.

A soft knock on the door pulls my attention.

"It's open." The door creaks open, and Julie, a club girl, walks in.

"You need some company?" No. Yes. I don't fucking know what I need. But instead of over-thinking it, I nod my head. Julie quickly starts to strip out of her clothes before standing in front of me naked. I motion for her to come to me and straddles my lap. I grab her face in my hands and press my lips to hers. I kiss her hard and rough, needing the outlet. She moans into my mouth, and I take it a step further. When I can't handle much more, I pull away and dump her onto the bed before pulling my clothes off in record time. With a condom in hand, I climb between her parted thighs and get comfortable.

She's in for a long fucking night.

CHAPTER SIX

I lean down and press my lips to Lance's before standing back up.

"Why do you have to go already?" he whines as I smile at him.

"I have other patients. You don't need me all day," I remind him.

"Yes, I do. I need you all the time." I've let Lance take me out a few times. It's been nice, and I've had a great time with him. Something just doesn't feel right, though. Something is missing, and I can't put my finger on it. He's super nice and sweet, but I feel like I need more. Something more. It isn't about the sex either. I don't need it, or at least that's what I'm telling myself because the man knows how to work his tongue just fine. I just feel like Lance is too good for me.

"You'll be fine, and I'll see you tomorrow," I tell him. He sighs as I smile and walk out of the room. His other nurse is just arriving, and we complete a handover before I head out the door.

I climb in my car and shove the key in, turning it, but nothing happens.

"What the hell?" I curse under my breath and try again. Nothing. It does nothing.

"What am I going to do?" I mumble to myself. I should buy a new car, but that's just more money I don't have. I call for a tow truck and sit back in the seat before dialing Shade's number.

"What?"

"Hey, it's Avery. I'm not going to make it today." I hate calling in. It makes me nauseous.

"Why the fuck not?"

"My car won't start. I'm stuck," I tell him the truth. I hear him mumbling on the other end before he finally speaks.

"Where are you? I'll pick you up," he says.

"You don't have to do that."

"I know that, but Bull needs you here. Where the hell are you?" I rattle off the address, and Shade hangs up. It takes about twenty minutes until the tow truck pulls up at the same time as Shade.

"Tow it here." He passes the guy a card.

"I have a local shop I use," I chime in. Shade rolls

his eyes and ignores me, talking to the driver. Then he turns back to me and nods toward his bike.

"I'm not riding that."

"Why not?"

"It's a death machine."

"No more than a car. Come on," he growls this time. I've noticed over our brief interactions that he's very growly. Shade passes me a helmet that I just stare at before he takes it away and places it on my head.

"Put that backpack on," he says, noticing the bag in my hand. I slip it on before he climbs on his bike and offers his hand. I throw my leg over the bike and climb on before securing my hands around his waist. I don't care that I barely know the man. I don't care if it hurts him either. I'm not letting go.

"You okay there?" he asks.

"I'm not falling off," I tell him. He chuckles, and it vibrates through me. Then he shifts and starts the bike, and I can feel his muscles shift under his shirt. And fuck does he smell good. I know I shouldn't be thinking of those things, but how can I not when I'm this close to him. The rumble of the bike isn't helping much either as I shift around the seat a little. Shade doesn't say anything, but I feel that rumble in his chest again. He's laughing at me.

Finally, he takes off, and we ride the twenty

minutes over to the clubhouse. I've never been on a bike before, but I must say that I didn't hate it. In fact, I liked it. More than I should.

"I'll take you home later and pick you up tomorrow," he says when he kills the engine and helps me off.

"You don't have to do that. I'll call a cab," I tell him.

"No, you won't. I said I'd take you." The aggravation in his tone is enough to make me stop arguing and nod my head at him.

"Okay. Thank you." He nods and motions toward the clubhouse. I take that as my hint and walk away.

When I step inside, I see the guys all standing around and a few girls hanging out by the bar, but then I see Bull in the back of the room. He doesn't notice me at first, and I take the time to examine him from a distance.

"You stalkin' him?" Shade asks over my shoulder.

"Just taking it all in. He's sad," I tell him.

"How do you know?"

"Look at him. The way his shoulders are slumped. You can tell a lot about a person by how they hold themselves. He'll put that happy mask back on when he sees me," I tell Shade.

"I don't think he does it. I think he's like that all the time," he argues. I don't think so. Bull finally looks up and straightens his shoulders, plastering a smile on his face.

"I told you." I walk away from Shade and head over to Bull, ready to work today.

"You look good today," he says as I step closer.

"Don't I every day?"

"Oh, you're teasin' me today, huh?"

"Is it working?"

"Not really. Do you mind if we skip today? I'm not really into it," he confirms what I already knew when I walked in.

"You have to do it."

"Listen, I get that you're the nurse and all but don't fuckin' boss me around, okay?"

"And I get that you're struggling today but don't give up. You have to work on this," I tell him. I can see the anger in his gaze before he lets his words fly.

"You don't see shit. You don't know what the fuck I feel right now. I said I'm not fuckin' doin' it today so go swish that pretty little ass of yours over to the goddamn bar and make yourself useful!" I take a step back and slam into someone. When I look over my shoulder, I see Shade seething with anger.

"What the fuck is this?"

"I don't feel like doin' shit today. Take nurse sexy ass over to the bar," Bull says.

"Don't talk to her like that, motherfucker. She's here to help your ass."

"And I don't want the goddamn help! Fuck off and leave me alone."

"Just because you're in that chair doesn't mean I won't beat the shit out of you," Shade growls as he steps around me. I raise my hand and press it to his chest before he stops. He looks at my hand before looking at my face, and I know I've crossed a line. I start to pull my hand away when he reaches up and grabs my wrist.

"Don't fuckin' move."

"What?"

"I said don't move," Shade repeats, then looks to Bull. "Apologize," he demands.

"Like fuck I will. I don't need this shit, Shade!"

"Fuckin' apologize, Bull, before I beat the fuck out of you!" Bull doesn't say shit, and that pisses Shade off even more. A few of the guys watch, but no one makes a move to step in. I beg with my eyes for someone to come over here, but they all stand their ground. Maybe it's because they're family that no one wants to intervene. I don't know what it is, but I wish they would stop it.

"Fuck you, brother. You want to go rounds with me, let's do it!" Bull roars. I try to pull my arm away from Shade's hurtful grasp, but he doesn't let go. He just holds on tighter.

"It's okay. He doesn't feel like it today. I'll come back tomorrow."

"I pay you for three hours. You'll be here for three hours," Shade grumbles. I nod my head, and finally, he releases me. I rub at my wrist as I look between the two.

"You know you're fuckin' it all up. She just wants to help."

"And I don't want help today, Shade. Not today." Shade finally nods his head, and I watch as Bull wheels himself away.

"I won't charge you for today," I tell him.

"You gotta get paid too. Come on," he says before he walks off. Shade takes long strides, and I try to keep up as best I can, but he's fast. Then he's at the bar, pouring two drinks. He slides one across the bar to me, and I shake my head.

"I can't drink on the job."

"You're off. Fuckin' drink it." I'm so confused by this man. Instead of arguing with him, I take the glass and bring it to my lips. I'm not much of a drinker, so it tastes like shit to me.

"I should probably go," I tell him.

"Scared of me?" he asks, raising an eyebrow. I should say no, but he is intimidating.

"Slightly." He smirks.

"Good. You should be."

CHAPTER SEVEN

SHADE

I should feel bad. At least a little, but I don't. I have a feeling that our little nurse hasn't let her hair down and had a good time in a very long time.

Now that she's drunk as fuck, she's dancing and laughing. I should feel bad, right? I mean, I did egg her on to drink more.

"What the hell did you do to her?" Ty asks when he comes to stand next to me.

"I don't think she was much of a drinker," I tell him.

"No shit. She's fuckin' wasted, brother."

"Not my fault."

"What the fuck do you mean not your fault? You gave it to her," he adds.

"I didn't know she wasn't a drinker."

"Better hope the little nurse can hold her liquor, or you're cleanin' that mess."

"Well, ain't this some shit," Mav says when he sees what's happening.

"What?"

"What'd you do?"

"Gave her a few drinks so she'd relax."

"It worked," he says, making me chuckle. Yeah, it sure as hell did work. She's drunk. Fucking drunk and dancing with the club girls. That wasn't really the plan. I just wanted her to relax and spend three hours thinking about something besides Bull and his attitude. Now she is.

I scrub my hand over my face and sigh when Ty nods to her taking her shirt off. I rush across the room and grab her arm, pulling her shirt back down.

"I think you're gettin' a little too happy, there," I tell her.

"What do you mean? I'm having a great time," she slurs as she presses her hands to my chest. There's something about this girl I like, but I can't put my finger on it. This could all end up badly for her or Bull, for that matter. He needs his nurse.

"I see that, but you need to keep your clothes on."

"I'd like to take yours off." She eyes me like I'm a piece of meat. Not that I mind, I love when a woman looks at me like that. I love when they're forward and willing, but this time is different. This is Bull's nurse, and I can't fuck that up for him.

"I bet you would, but you can't do that. It's gettin' late. Think you should go home," I tell her.

"The fun has only just started," she whines, pressing that sexy little body of hers against mine. I could push her away, but I don't want to. Instead, I pull her closer, letting my body slam against hers.

"You're so hard," she whispers as I chuckle. I grab her hand and bring it to my cock, and she moans.

"My body isn't the only thing that's hard," I tell her.

"You like me."

"I do like you," I tell her as she squeezes slightly. "But we can't do that."

"Why?" Her whines are sexy as fuck. They go straight to my cock.

"Because you're here for my cousin," I admit to her.

"I'm only his nurse. Nothing more."

"And he needs you to keep bein' his nurse." She nods her head as I pull away from her and grab Julie. I drag her around in front of me and shove her to her knees while Avery watches. Julie knows the drill and pulls my hard cock free from my jeans before licking the tip. Then she sucks me into her mouth, and I nearly groan. Wrapping my hand up in her hair, I help her along as Avery stares at me. Her eyes move from Julie and my cock up to meet my eyes, and I see the hurt in them. I should stop this. I shouldn't do this to her, in front of her. But I'm a bastard. I'm an asshole who doesn't care what she thinks at the moment. I shove Julie's head further, and she takes me deeper before I feel that tingle and release. I come down the back of her throat, groaning as I do.

"Why did you do that?" Avery asks softly.

"Because you couldn't do it," I tell her. She steps toward me, pulling my cock from Julie's mouth and rubbing the length of it.

"I could have done it so much better than her," she slurs, and my cock jerks in her hand. Avery smiles, and it's breathtaking. Then something must hit her because she steps back and lets her grip fall away from me.

"I need to go." She heads for the door as I tuck my cock back into my jeans and follow her.

"You're drunk," I remind her.

"I don't give a fuck. I need to go."

"You're not goin' anywhere like this."

"Well, I'm not staying here," she argues.

"What the hell is with you?" I ask, grabbing her

shoulder and spinning her to face me. Anger dances in her pretty brown eyes.

"What is with me? You just had some girl sucking you off, and you think I have a problem?" Her hands are on her hips as she glares at me. It's about that time that Bull comes back out and right up next to us.

"What's happenin'?"

"Your cousin is an ass," she yells.

"I knew that much. What'd he do? Are you drunk?" Bull asks.

"She is drunk."

"I'm not that drunk!" she slurs as Bull chuckles.

"You got my nurse drunk?" he asks, looking up at me.

"A little."

"Damn, baby. Come here," Bull says. Avery sighs and walks over, leaning down in Bull's face. He whispers something to her that I can't hear, but she laughs and nods her head. Then I see him pull her to him, kissing her. Something inside of me wants to uncoil and break them apart, but I can't do that. I won't do that to him. I've put him through enough hell. But then I don't have to. Avery pulls away first and shakes her head.

"We can't do this," she tells him. "I need to go."

"I'll take you home." She looks over at me and

nods her head. I pull my keys from my pocket and nod for the door. She walks over and takes one last look at Bull before she walks out.

"I'll be back," I tell him before following her outside.

I help her in the truck before I walk around and climb in. She looks lost in her head but rattles off her address. I put the truck in drive and pull out of the parking lot, heading in the direction she told me. I can tell she's debating what happened back there. Something is at war within her.

The drive doesn't take long, and I pull into her driveway and put the truck in park. Avery just sits there, not saying a word until she finally unbuckles and throws herself into my lap. Her ass hits the horn before she readjusts herself and grinds against my cock. Her lips are on mine, kissing me as if her life depends on it, and I let her. Fuck I shouldn't, but I do.

"What are you doin'?" I ask in between her kisses.

"I'm drunk and horny."

"And you're gonna regret this later," I tell her. She doesn't say anything, just lifts and pulls my cock free of my jeans. Then she's stroking it, and fuck do I like it.

"Avery," I warn her, but she doesn't stop. Instead,

she's lifting herself and pulling her pants off, shoving them to the side. I've never seen anyone as turned on as she is right now. She pulls her panties to the side and slowly positions herself over me before sliding down my length with a moan.

"What the hell are you doin'?" I ask her as she rides my cock right here in her driveway.

"I need this. I need you," Avery moans as she takes me harder. I don't complain. I just know it's all fucking wrong, but that doesn't mean I'm going to stop her. I'm not. I grip her hips and hold on for the fucking ride. Her lips claim mine in a kiss that would shake any man. Her tongue dips into my mouth, toying with mine as her hips rise and fall. The faster she goes, the harder I get. Then I feel her clench, and she bites my lip until I taste blood.

"Fuck me," I growl as I raise my hips to meet hers. Then we're both falling apart. Tumbling over the invisible line of pleasure as I fill her full of me. Her head drops onto my shoulder as she shudders.

"Don't regret this later," I tell her.

"I won't."

"When you're sober, you will."

"No, I don't think so."

"What the fuck?" I hear someone yell. Fuck, someone saw us fucking in the driveway. Avery's head lifts quickly, and she looks around before climbing off my lap. She quickly pulls her clothes on as I see another man in a wheelchair near the window. Jesus. He watched us fuck? What kind of sick son of a bitch is he?

I climb out of the truck, ready to take his ass on with Avery close behind me.

"Lance. What are you doing here?" she asks as she adjusts her clothes.

"You were watchin' us fuck? Did you get yourself off, asshole?" I growl at him.

"I could ask you the same. I thought you were coming over after work, Avery. Now I see what you've been doing," the man snarls.

"It's not like that. I've been drinking and ..."

"And it just happened?" the guy asks.

"I'm sorry, Lance."

"You should be. This is done. This is over."

"Lance, please," she says as tears fill her eyes. I walk over and grab her, kissing her like my life depends on it this time. I slide my tongue into her mouth and take what I want because, from this second on, she's mine. I don't give a fuck if she was drunk or not. I'm claiming her ass as my own, and fuck the consequences.

"What the hell?" The man roars. I ignore him. I keep kissing her until her legs begin to shake, and I have to hold her ass up. I hear a car door slam, and before I know it, he's gone. Then I pull away from her and smirk.

"Why did you do that?"

"Because you aren't fuckin' him anymore."

"What? What do you mean? I'm so confused."

"You aren't fuckin' him anymore."

"I wasn't fucking him. We were dating."

"Not anymore," I repeat.

"What do you mean? You can't tell me who I can date."

"I just did. Go in and clean up. I'll see you tomorrow."

"No. Fuck that. Wait a minute, Shade." I stand with my arms crossed over my chest, glaring at her.

"What?"

"You can't just do this. You can't tell me I'm not dating him anymore."

"I'm pretty sure fuckin' me in the driveway fixed that for you."

"Don't be an asshole!"

"Don't be stupid. I just said you're not to fuck him or date him anymore. End of subject."

"No, it is not. You're not my boss." I move now, stepping into her space. I lower my head, so we're at eye level.

"You wanna fuck? I'll fuck you. You wanna date? I'll take you. You're not fuckin' anyone else."

"We're not together, Shade. I barely know you."

"And that didn't stop you from ridin' my cock in the truck. You'll get to know me. Now go inside and clean up. The thought of my cum runnin' down your pretty little thighs is makin' me hard again. Unless you want me to fuck you one more time?" It's a question. I'll let her answer, but I know that she doesn't want to. She's too confused right now, and I don't blame her. I just dropped a fucking bomb on her.

I help Bull in a daze. It's been a few days since the shit happened with Shade. I should be embarrassed, but I'm not. I should feel bad, but I don't. I enjoyed myself. The only thing I do feel bad about is Lance. He didn't deserve that, but he also shouldn't have shown up at my house either.

"You okay?" Bull asks as I lift his leg and place it back on the floor.

"I'm fine."

"This about the other day? You can let loose and have fun here, Avery. Not everything has to be work," he tells me. I smile and nod my head.

"It's not that. I shouldn't have been drinking, but your cousin is a little persuasive."

"You got a thing for Shade?" he asks. I shake my

head. No way in hell would I tell him that, not after he kissed me.

"No."

"It's okay if you do."

"Is it?" I ask and see the look in his eyes. It's not okay because I think Bull is starting to feel things for me, and that's only going to end badly.

"It is. I mean, he's a good guy," he tells me.

"He might be, but he isn't my type."

"What is your type?" he asks as I work on his legs.

"I don't know, really. A guy who works hard and does his best. I don't think I have a specific type," I admit.

"I work hard."

"Yeah, you do. And I'm proud of you over the last few days. You've done amazing work."

"But?"

"But I don't feel that for you, Bull. I really don't."

"But you feel somethin' for Shade?" How do I answer that?

"Stop questionin' my woman." Shade's deep voice booms through the room. I turn and look over my shoulder to see him standing in the doorway.

"Your woman?" Bull asks.

"Yeah. Claimin' her ass," Shade retorts. I don't

know what the hell that means, but I shove to my feet and shake my head.

"I'm sober now, and we're not doing this," I tell him.

"Doin' what?"

"This claiming thing you're talking about."

"Can't change it now," Bull adds.

"He's right. We don't just claim things on a daily basis."

"What the hell does that even mean?" I snap at him. Shade comes toward me while Bull laughs. I don't know what the hell is happening here, but I don't like it.

He steps into my space, grabbing my face in his hands before leaning down to my level.

"It means you're mine. No one else will be fuckin' you but me. No one else will touch you but me. You get it now?"

"What?"

"You heard me."

"You're insane!" I snap, pulling away from him. Bull doesn't stop laughing, and that pisses me off even more. I should slap him for that. I should take my anger out on someone, but Bull doesn't deserve it.

"You're delusional if you think that's how it's going to work," I say as Shade stands to full height. I don't care how menacing he looks. I'm not backing down. He isn't running my life for me.

"You are if you think you can fight me on this," he says. I push at his chest and scream.

"You can't fuck up my life!"

"He already did," Bull laughs once more.

"You aren't telling me what to do and who to do it with."

"I already told you," Shade says calmly.

"Well, you're wrong," I snap at him.

"No, I think he's right," Bull adds. I spin around to face him now.

"What is your problem? Do you think this shit is funny?" he laughs harder.

"I think it's damn funny. He just claimed your ass," he says, laughing more. What the hell is with these two?

"What did I just hear?" Another guy, Tyrant, walks in and asks.

"Shade is claimin' my nurse."

"No, he's not!"

"Yeah, he is. He already said it, Prez. Looks like we're gettin' a new old lady around here."

"A what? I'm not going to be some old lady around here," I tell them.

"So let me get this straight. You're claimin' the nurse?" Tyrant asks, looking at Shade.

"Looks that way."

"And she don't want it?"

"She doesn't know what she wants yet," Shade says.

"Like fuck I don't! I said no."

"Here's the thing around here, Avery. You don't get to say no. Now I get that this is new to you, but you'll get used to it." Tyrant explains. Bullshit. I'm not getting used to anything. Fuck that. Just as the thought crosses my mind, I hear noises firing off. Glass shatters before Shade is tossing my ass to the floor. Bull throws himself out of his chair and lands next to us.

"What the hell, Shade?" Bull roars.

"Stay with her," he tells Bull as he stands to his feet and rushes from the room with Tyrant.

"What's happening?" I ask Bull.

"Someone is shootin' at the clubhouse," he answers casually as if this happens all the time. What the hell is wrong with these people?

"Shooting?"

"Yeah. Don't know much else as you can see." I stay down, but I don't hear any more shots. A few minutes later, Shade strolls back in with a smirk on his face. He walks over and lifts Bull back into his chair before looking at me, still lying on the ground.

"Get up." I don't move. Then he's walking over and yanking me off the ground and to my feet.

"You can't just yank me around like that."

"Yeah, I can."

"No, you can't."

"What was it?" Bull asks, changing the subject.

"Fuckin' prospects," he replies as I stand here unsure what to do.

"What the hell does that mean?"

"The prospects were just havin' a little fun. It got out of hand," Shade says as if it's nothing. Is he insane? He needs help!

"Having fun? Someone could have been killed."

"You ain't dead." He looks me over. My mouth drops open before I stomp out of the room and out toward the bar. I grab the first bottle I can find when I hear Bull laughing.

"You broke my nurse," he declares, watching me take down as much as I can before it hits me.

"Is this normal for you?" I ask, looking between him and Shade.

"Pretty much. The prospects get a little out of hand."

"A little out of hand? They shot at us!"

"They weren't shootin' at us. They were shootin' at the side of the buildin'. He has bad aim," Shade brushes it off as nothing.

"They shot at us!"

"No, they didn't." I don't know why I feel like a hysterical mess, but I do. I set the drink down and head for the door when Shade grabs my wrist and jerks me back.

"Where the hell do you think you're goin'?"

"Um, home! Where I won't be shot at!"

"You just drank," he reminds me.

"No shit, I could have died," I tell him as Bull chuckles.

"You weren't going to die," Bull adds.

"How the hell do you know that?"

"You're feisty today," he says, pissing me off a little more.

"I was just shot at."

"They weren't shootin' at you," Shade repeats his earlier words. I don't give a shit if they are dumb as hell and shooting at the clubhouse. I'm inside the fucking clubhouse.

"I don't need this shit. I don't get paid enough for this," I mumble under my breath.

"She needs a raise, Shade. You ain't payin' her enough," Bull laughs. I'm glad to see him smiling and getting some kind of enjoyment out of this.

"I'm not payin' her to whine," Shade says.

"Whine? How close was that bullet to me?" I snap at him.

"I think she needs to be fucked," Bull announces. Shade steps closer, pressing his body against mine.

"Is that what it is? You need my cock deep inside you again?"

"Again?" Bull asks curiously.

"Our little drunken nurse got horny as hell when I was dropping her off," Shade says, causing my cheeks to heat. Is he really telling him that?

"Oh shit. That's what made you claim her ass?"

"Somethin' like that."

"Damn, Shade."

"What?" he asks as I look between all of them.

"Are you all fucking insane?" I squeal.

"No." Both of them answer at the same time.

"You have people shooting at the place you live in. That's not a concern?" I ask, looking around the room as other guys come strolling in as if nothing happened. A few laugh, while others just smile.

"They weren't a rival," Shade adds.

"And that makes it okay?" I ask, unsure what the hell he's saying.

"Pretty much."

"I'm going home."

"No, you're not. You've been drinkin' again."

"That seems to be a theme around here," Bull says. I roll my eyes and look at Shade.

"You said you were taking me home. I want to go now."

"Our day isn't over," Bull laughs at me. I flip him off, knowing damn good and well this is unprofessional of me, but I was just shot at. That isn't very professional either. Shade wraps his hands around my hips and tugs me closer to him. I gasp as he slides his hand up my sides and finally around my neck.

"Stop bossin' me around. You aren't the boss here, Avery. I am."

"I don't care. I didn't sign up for this shit," I tell him. He smirks at me, and damn it, Shade looks perfect.

"You have another hour with my cousin." I swallow hard and let that sink in. He's right. I've never been one to skip out on my work. I nod my head, and he grins before pulling away. I turn on my heel and walk toward the gym before motioning for Bull to follow me.

"I think that went well," Bull declares as he follows me back into his room.

"I think that's bullshit," I grumble.

SHADE

I don't know what it is about her attitude I like, but I do. Now I sit here with Bull drinking a beer while he looks at me like he has something to say.

"What about Addy?" Bull asks, pissing me off. I tip my drink to my lips and take another long pull.

"What about her?"

"You can't just bring a new woman in and not introduce her."

"That's exactly what I'm doin'. Addy doesn't need this shit. She's happy where she is."

"With your mom and dad?"

"It is what it is, Bull. Don't start this shit," I tell him.

"Don't you think she deserves her dad?"

"I see her on the weekends," I remind him.

"Oh, for fucks sake. You still blame yourself,

don't you?" How could I not? I know what I did. I know what happened to Addy's mom was because of me.

"It was my fault," I remind him.

"She died by your hands?" he asks, pissing me off further.

"Not my hands, but it might as well have been."

"Addy needs you, man. She needs her dad."

"Don't tell me what the fuck she needs. What she needed was her mom, and now she'll never have that."

"So fuckin' the nurse fixes that?" he pushes. I take another long pull of my beer and flip him off. "You think findin' a new bitch will fix everything?"

"No. I don't. I can't fix what I've done."

"Then what the hell is this shit? What are you doin'?"

"What are you bitches arguin' about?" Cowboy asks as he drops into the seat next to me.

"Addy."

"What about her? She okay?" They all worry about her. They all know she's okay with my parents, though.

"She's fine."

"Then what are we talkin' about?"

"The fact that this motherfucker needs to man up and be her father," Bull tells him.

"You've been a patch for all of a minute, Bull. Don't think I won't fuck you up," I remind him.

"No, you won't."

"Try me, motherfucker."

"You into beatin' on the disabled now?" he asks. I flip him off once more.

"What does any of this have to do with Addy?" Cowboy asks, confused by the whole situation. Hell, I'm not far behind him. I don't know why Bull wants to push the issue, but he is.

"I'm just sayin' if I had a kid, I'd want to be around it," Bull says.

"You don't have a kid," I remind him.

"No shit, and I never fuckin' will, man. Get your head out of your ass and be that girls father!" He snaps before wheeling away from the table. I sit back with my drink in hand and wonder what the hell his issue is. Is he really that pissed about not having kids? Is that what's bothering him?

"That was intense," Cowboy says.

"No shit."

"What's gotten into him?"

"Apart from the fact that I'm fuckin' his nurse?"

"Well, there is that," he chuckles.

"I think it's all sinkin' in now. The fact that he can't have kids or walk. I think it's all startin' to hit him at once."

"Might be. Maybe he's right, though. It's been a year, and you haven't brought Addy around here."

"She's a baby. And look what the prospects just did. You think a child should be here?"

"You know damn good and well that shit wouldn't happen if there were kids around."

"Probably not," I agree. In fact, I know it wouldn't. The prospects would be stationed outside the clubhouse watching over things if there were kids here.

"It just hurts to look at her," I admit to him.

"I get that. I do, but you can't hide from the past, brother."

"I can, and I will. She's thrivin' with them. I don't want to fuck that up," I tell him.

"You barely see her."

"What the fuck is this shit? Rag on me day? What the hell did I do to you motherfuckers?" I'm beyond pissed. I'm aggravated by all of this. I don't bring her around because I don't want to. I don't want to look at her and feel bad. I don't want to see her mom in her eyes, but I do.

"What happened to Jenny isn't on you, Shade."

"It is on me. Fuck!" I slam my beer onto the table in front of me. I stand to my feet and stalk through the clubhouse and down to my room. I don't need this shit. I don't need a reminder of what happened.

Once I'm in my room, I head into the bathroom, turning the shower on. I strip out of my clothes and climb in, not caring that it isn't warm yet. The cold water hits me, and I sigh as I run my hand through my hair. I'm not in here long when I hear someone in my room. I swear to god, if it's Bull, I'm going to beat his ass. I don't feel like dealing with him anymore today. I climb out of the shower and wrap a towel around my waist. Walking into my room, I see her standing with her arms crossed over her chest.

"What the hell are you doin' here?"

"Bull thought you might need someone to talk to," she says softly.

"I don't need to talk," I tell her. Avery nods her head as she stares at me. "Are you just gonna stand there and stare at me?"

"What else should I do?"

"Leave."

"He's worried about you."

"He doesn't need to be. Bull needs to worry about himself," I tell her. Water trickles down my chest, and her eyes follow it. I lick my lips before running my hand through my hair, pulling her attention.

"I'm a good listener," she says. I take a step toward her and watch as her body slowly tenses.

"I bet you're good at other stuff too."

"Like what?" she asks softly. I step toward her, and she backs against the wall. I keep going until there's only a breath between us.

"I bet you're good at suckin' cock." Her cheeks heat as I reach up and glide my fingers along her cheek. I see the way she shudders, and I know she wants me the way I want her. I press my body against hers, and she leans in, licking the water drops off my chest. I growl low in my throat before grabbing the back of her neck and forcing her to look up at me. I lower my head and brush my lips over her. Just the slight taste of her causes my cock to stir.

"What are you doing?" she asks.

"Takin' what belongs to me," I reply before slamming my lips against hers. Our kiss is heated, passionate, and full of lust. Avery wants this. I know she does. I pin her against the wall, shoving her legs apart with mine. I grind my cock against her as she moans into my mouth. I reach between us and loosen the towel, letting it fall to the floor. Her hand comes in between us, grabbing my cock in her hand. She strokes me hard until she causes me to groan loudly. Then I pull my lips from hers and shove her to her knees. She falls to the floor in front of me and leans in. I look down, keeping my eyes on her as she slides the tip of my cock into her mouth. I keep my hand on the back of her neck, guiding her. I rock my hips, shoving my cock into the back of her throat. She gags, and tears come to her pretty eyes. I grin and bite my lip between my teeth as she sucks me harder.

"Just like that," I encourage her as she continues to suck. Her tongue slides along my shaft, and I moan. Gripping the back of her neck harder, I thrust into her mouth. I fuck her face hard and fast until I feel her nails digging into my thighs. She tries to pull away from me, but I don't let her. I buck my hips harder and shoot my load down the back of her throat. Avery gags but swallows until I finish pulling out of her mouth.

"Damn, baby. I didn't know it'd be that good," I tell her as I tug her to her feet. She stares at me, unblinking for a long second.

"What do you want with me?" she asks.

"What do you mean?"

"You make it a point to say you've claimed me in front of everyone. What do you want with me?"

"What's the difference?" I ask her. She huffs out a breath before turning on her heel and walking away from me. I chuckle and watch her go before pulling my clothes on.

CHAPTER TEN

AVERY

Work has been work, but this thing with Shade has been wearing on me. I don't know what the hell he wants with me; I think it's all about the sex. But that doesn't stop me from showing up to do my job with Bull, though.

"You're off today," he speaks as I sit on the bench and look over at him.

"You're doing really well. You might not need me for much longer," I tell him.

"Don't change the subject," he says as I let out a sigh.

"I don't know what to say, Bull. Your cousin has my head a mess."

"He's good at that."

"He just wants sex," I tell him.

"I don't know if that's all he wants," Bull chimes in.

"It is. That's what this shit is to him. He isn't looking for a relationship."

"AND YOU ARE?"

"I was dating someone. It was nice, but something was missing. Then your cousin shows up and ruins that."

"You weren't happy anyway," he tells me. He's right. I wasn't that happy with Lance. We had fun, but that's about it.

"Does that matter?"

"It must, or you wouldn't be lettin' Shade use that pussy." His laughter pisses me off. This isn't funny. I didn't ask to be in a relationship or whatever the hell this thing is between Shade and me.

"I don't know what this is," I confess.

"What are you two doin'?" Speak of the devil, and he shall appear.

"We're talkin' shit about you. She needs answers," Bull replies as I slap at his arm. He chuckles before shrugging his shoulders. "It's true."

"What answers?"

"She wants to know what this shit is between you two."

"What shit between us?" Shade asks. I shove off the bench and head for the door, not ready to deal with this shit today. I can't. I'm frustrated and on edge. But, of course, I don't get that far. His hand grips my wrist, and he pulls me back in front of him.

"Don't walk away from me."

"Don't pull on me."

"I can do whatever I want with you. You're mine."

"This is stupid," I smart off.

"I didn't ask you. I said you were mine," he growls.

"Yours to what? Fuck when you please? You won't even talk to me!" I'm exasperated, and I'm pissed off. I'm in a bad mood, and this isn't helping. I need more from him. I need ... just more.

"I have a daughter." What? His words weren't what I expected to hear.

"You do?"

"She's a year old."

"Where is she?"

"This, Avery, is why I don't want to talk to you. We click. We fuck. It works."

"I need more than that," I tell him. He nods his head before Bull rolls past us in his wheelchair.

"She lives with my parents. I can't take care of her."

"Why not?"

"Look around. This is the life I live." He's making no sense. Of course, there are a few issues with having a child here, but from what I know about these guys, they'd do anything for their families. That little girl is family.

"I am looking. I see a family. I see people who care about each other more than most blood families do. What am I missing?"

"Her mom."

"Where is she? Are you still with her? Damn it, Shade, if you were fucking me while you have a wife, I swear to god."

"She's dead," he cuts me off of my little rant.

"I'm sorry," I apologize softly, not sure what else to say.

"I'm the reason she's dead."

"What do you mean?"

"I pushed her away. I couldn't deal with her cheatin' and shit. She begged me to take her back, and I said no. Her new boyfriend beat her to death. My little girl was there. She was only a month old."

"Jesus. I don't know what to say."

"You wanted more? Well, there it is." He pulls away from me and tries to walk off, but it's my turn to stop him.

"Wait," I call after him. He slowly stops, his head dropping forward before he turns to face me.

"I don't want your pity," he says, looking me in the eye. That's not what I was doing. Instead of saying it, I walk toward him, grab his face in my hands and kiss the fuck out of him. I don't know what it is about him that makes me feel safe and secure. I don't know why the hell I feel this connection to him, but I do. And it drives me crazy. It makes me insane, but I want to see what's under all his scars. I want to see the man who he was made to be. I want it all, and I'm a greedy bitch.

"What's that for?"

"I want you too, Shade."

"Do you?" I nod my head before his lips take over. His kiss seers me to my core.

"You think the stars will align for us, Avery?" I look him in the eye and see just how serious he is about this. I shrug my shoulders before pulling his lips back to mine. In this moment, I don't care what aligns as long as he doesn't stop kissing me.

"What made you change your mind?" Shade asks when he pulls back.

"Everything. I want everything."

"And you think I'm gonna give it to you?"

"I don't know. We can always hope," I tell him.

CHAPTER ELEVEN

SHADE

I'm nervous about this. I'm not sure I should be doing it, but it doesn't matter now. We're almost there. There is no turning back after this.

Avery looks over at me but doesn't say a word. I can feel her gaze on me. I didn't tell her where we were going. I didn't want to spend the entire drive listening to her question me.

I pull into the driveway and park, killing the engine of the truck. My stomach is in knots, just like it always is when I come over here. I'm nervous about what Avery is going to say and how she will react to all this.

I climb out of the truck and walk around, opening her door and helping her out. She still doesn't speak as I grab her hand in mine and pull her along with me.

"You're not going to say anything? Just throw me to the wolves?" she finally speaks up. I nod my head and raise my hand to knock on the door. Avery tries to move away from me, but I don't let her. Instead, I hold her tighter.

"You can't do this to me," she says as the door opens. My mom smiles when she sees me but not when she looks over at Avery.

"Mom, this is Avery. Avery, this is my mom."

"It's nice to meet you," Avery says politely as my mom takes her in. Then she offers her hand, and they shake quickly before my mom ushers us inside. I can tell Avery is uncomfortable, and I don't care. She wanted to know me, and now she's about to.

"Where's Addy?" I ask.

"In there with your dad. She's fussy today," mom replies as I drag Avery along into the living room. My dad looks up and says hello to both of us before Addy sees me. Her little eyes light up as she takes me in before a toothy grin breaks out across her face. Her arms rise, waiting for me to pick her up. Reluctantly I release my grip on Avery and walk over, picking up my daughter.

"What are you doin', baby girl?" I ask as she squeals with happiness.

"We'll leave you guys alone for a while."

"Would you pack her a bag? We're takin' her out

a for a while." My mom's face breaks into a grin I haven't seen in a long time as she nods her head rapidly. They both leave the room when Avery walks over and smiles at my daughter.

"So this is her?" she asks, running her fingers along her cheek.

"This is Addy. My daughter."

"She's beautiful, Shade. Looks like you."

"Spittin' image of me. My mom likes to compare baby pictures of us." This is weird. It's strange having a woman around Addy, but this is what Avery wanted. This is what she needed.

"She's perfect."

"She is."

"How could you walk away from this?" she asks softly as she continues to rub Addy's cheek and hair.

"How could I not? She deserves more than I can give her."

"I think you're wrong. I think you're scared of her."

"I'm not scared of her."

"Yes, you are. Addy is a reminder of your past."

"She has her eyes. I see her in them every fuckin' time I see her."

"Shade. You can't live like that. Look at her," Avery tells me. I look down at my daughter, and I can't do anything when my chest clenches.

"It's not that easy."

"It kind of is, Shade. She needs her dad."

"She needs a family who will take care of her and love her. She has that here," I tell her.

"No. That isn't what she has. You're her family," she snaps at me.

"I didn't bring you here for your mouth!"

"Then what the hell did you bring me here for?" she yells a little louder.

"I don't know what this is between you two, but she doesn't need to hear it," my mom says as she walks into the room with Addy's car seat and bag. I look over at her and nod, knowing she doesn't need to hear us arguing.

"Sorry."

"What do you want from me, Shade?" Avery finally asks. My mom leaves the room as I turn to face her fully.

"You wanted to know me. That includes knowin' Addy even if she isn't with me all the time."

"I don't know that I can accept that." She's confusing me.

"What do you mean?"

"I'm not sure I can be with a man who doesn't even want to keep his child. I'm okay with the fact you have a daughter, but you're not with her all the time, Shade. You might love her, but you don't take care of her, and that's a huge turn-off for me. I want to go home."

"We're takin' Addy out today."

"I'm not doing this. Take me home." I huff out a breath before placing Addy in her car seat. Grabbing her bag and the handle, I head for the door with Avery right behind me. If she thinks for one second that I'm taking her after she wanted this, she has another thing coming.

We head out to the truck, and I strap Addy in. Avery climbs in the front but spins around to look over the seat. She talks baby talk to Addy, and I love that she laughs and giggles at her. I start the truck up and pull out of the driveway while her words gnaw at my insides. I shouldn't take her words to heart, but I am.

Shaking the thoughts away, I drive to the local park and pull in a parking spot.

"I said I wanted to go home."

"And I said no." I climb out, ignoring her huffs and complaints as I grab Addy from her seat and head toward the swings. I slide her little legs through the baby swing and give her a little push. She squeals in delight, and it makes my heart swell.

"Why are you doing this?"

"I already told you. You wanted to know my life so bad. This is it." She shoves the swing a little when it starts to slow down. Addy claps her hands and laughs her little heart out, and it fills mine with joy. I can't lie and say I hate when I'm around her. It's the opposite. I love being with Addy. I love when she smiles at me. I love everything about that baby. I just don't know how to be with her all the time and not remember what I caused.

"She was young, her mom. She was unrecognizable when they found her."

"It wasn't your fault," she tells me, just like everyone else has. In my right mind, I know she's right.

"It's hard not to take the blame. I sent Jenny away. I didn't want her around," I admit.

"She did what she wanted to do. You can't take all the blame, Shade."

"I'll try harder," I tell her.

"What do you mean?"

"With Addy. I'll try harder." Just as the words leave my mouth, I hear people screaming. When I look up, I'm hit in the face with something hard. My vision blurs as I try to blink to regain my sight. Avery is running toward the truck with Addy in her arms as I stumble and look around. That's when I see the Demon Raiders MC.

CHAPTER TWELVE

AVERY

Everything happened so quickly. Those men surrounded Shade, and one hit him with a pipe. I knew right then I needed to get that baby out of there. I grabbed her and ran toward the truck, which is where we now sit. I'm out of breath and scared to death. Grabbing my cell phone, I dial Bull.

"Yeah?"

"Something's happened. I don't know what to do!"

"What the hell are you talkin' about?"

"I'm so scared! They grabbed him, Bull!"

"Who grabbed who? Calm down, Avery." I watch as they drag an unconscious Shade into the back of a van as tears fall down my cheeks.

"We were at the park with Addy. Some guys came

out of nowhere and hit him and took him, Bull. They took him!" The baby cries in the background, but all I can focus on is the van pulling away quickly. My god, why didn't I help him? What kind of person does that make me? I let them hurt him. Regret and shame spear me to the core. I should have done something.

"I didn't help him, Bull. What the hell is wrong with me?"

"Where are you, Avery?"

"In the truck."

"Listen to me. I need you to get that baby back here, do you hear me? You both need to get back to the clubhouse. I'm callin' Tyrant, okay?"

"They just took him!" I cry harder.

"We'll get him back. Just get here, okay? Can you do that?" I nod my head as I buckle the baby into her seat and situate myself in the driver's seat. I adjust the seat before swallowing hard and starting the truck, thankful that he passed me the keys to begin with.

"Stay calm, Avery," Bull instructs as I sit the phone on the console next to me. I take a deep breath as the baby screams louder.

"She's so upset," I cry with her.

"She'll be fine. Get here. I'm gonna hang up now. Okay?"

"Okay." With a few more deep breathes, I try to calm my nerves and talk to Addy as I drive.

"It's okay, Addy. Daddy is going to be okay. We're going to see uncle Bull. Would you like that?" I talk to her as calmly as possible as I drive toward the clubhouse. My heart is racing, blood pounding in my ears. I take a few more calming breathes and keep talking to Addy as she slowly calms in the back. My heart feels like it may beat out of my chest.

The drive to the clubhouse seems to take forever when in reality, it's only been minutes. Ten at the most. I pull into the parking lot seeing all the guys, including Bull, waiting outside for me. When I climb out, I move to the back seat to grab Addy.

"What happened? I need details." Tyrant doesn't waste any time. I cradle the now sleeping baby in my arms as he leads me inside. Then he leads me into one of the offices off to the side of the main room.

"I need to know what happened."

"We were just standing there talking and pushing her on the swing. These guys came out of nowhere and hit him with a pipe. I was so scared, I grabbed the baby and ran," I tell them as tears fill my eyes. "I was a coward. I shouldn't have left him."

"You did the right thing. He would have lost it if anything happened to Addy," Tyrant says.

"I left him," I hiss at him.

"You did the right thing, Avery. Did you get a look at the guys?"

"They were wearing cuts like yours. There were five of them. They had a van," I tell them what I can remember.

"They were wearin' cuts? Did you see anything on them?" I shake my head as I try to remember and look down at the sleeping baby in my arms. What is happening? Do I take her back to her grandparents? What happens now?

"Avery?"

"I ... it had a monster or devil or something on the back riding a motorcycle," I tell him.

"Fuckin' Demon Raiders," Tyrant growls.

"What?"

"Nothin' for you to worry about. You good with the baby, or you want me to get one of the girls to take her?"

"No, I got her. What's happening? Why did they take him?"

"It's club business, Avery. Take the baby to Shade's room."

"You can't just do that to me. I was there."

"I know you were, and if they saw you, they may be after you now. You and that baby are stayin' here."

"I have to work! Shade is missing! This is insane," I snap at him. I know I shouldn't, but I can't help myself. It's all too much. My heart hurts as I look down at the baby in my arms. It's her dad.

"What do I tell her grandparents?"

"I'll take care of that," Bull answers as he rolls into the room. I nod my head, unsure what to do. I know they said to take her back to the room, but then what? What do I do then? I ran. I didn't try to help him, but all I could think about was this baby. What if someone hurt the baby? Those were the only thoughts running through my head.

"Avery, I need you to relax. You're safe now," Bull tries to calm me as he recognizes my inner turmoil.

"They just took him, Bull."

"We'll get him back. Just calm down, okay." I nod my head as I turn and walk out of the room, heading for the bedroom as I was told to do. My body still shakes from the sobs that won't stop coming, and I can't control them.

When I step into his room, I break down a little more; it smells like him. When did this man start meaning so much to me? When did things change? I ask myself a million questions as I cradle Addy to my chest. Knowing she needs to sleep, I lay her down in the middle of the bed, pulling the blanket over her. She stirs but quickly falls back asleep when the door opens, and Bull comes in. He looks from Addy to me before motioning me to follow him. I take one last look at the sleeping baby and follow him into the hallway.

"I dealt with my aunt and uncle. You did the right thing takin' her and runnin' Avery. It might not seem like it now, but Shade would have lost his mind if that baby had been hurt."

"He was so helpless. I feel so bad," I tell him.

"Don't do that. He's tough, strong. Shade can handle whatever they throw at him. That baby wouldn't stand a chance," he reminds me. I nod my head even though there's an ache in my chest. One that can't be fixed or taken away.

"What happens now?"

"We try to figure out what they want and where they have him."

"What do they want?" I ask more to myself than to him.

"We don't know. They've always wanted control of our area, but it could be anything at this point. We'll figure it out." His voice is calm, as if he isn't about to snap himself. I can see the look in his eyes. I can sense the shift in him. He's as pissed as I am. Probably more.

"How do we handle this? With the baby and all?"

"I'll get one of the girls to take care of her," he says.

"No. I'll do it. I can't go to work anyway. I want to do it," I tell him. Bull nods and looks up at me.

"Ty is gettin' some baby gear brought in. A bed and things like that. She'll have whatever she needs here."

"And the shooting shit? That won't happen again, will it?"

"No. Not with Addy here. Nothin' is gonna happen now that she's here, Avery."

"Okay. Good."

"You sure you want to take care of her?"

"I'm sure. I think I need to."

"Don't put this on yourself, Avery. You can't do that."

"Do you know Shade blames himself for you?" I change the subject.

"I know, and I could kick his ass for it. I chose to go out that day."

"I don't know all the details, but I know enough. He's a good guy, Bull."

"He is. And you can tell him that when we get his ass back." I smile, but it doesn't reach my eyes. Will they get him back? I don't know how their world works. I don't know what those men wanted with him. I don't know if I'll ever see him again.

CHAPTER THIRTEEN

Black. Pitch fucking black. That's all I see. My ears ring from the hit to the head, but it's the pitch black that's getting to me. I can't see my fucking hand in front of my face. I can't see anything. So I feel. I feel around to try and figure out where the hell I am. All I feel is concrete under me and what feels like cell bars around me. I growl as I keep feeling around. I find what I assume to be a toilet, but that's it. There's nothing else in this cell. Not a damn thing.

My mind shifts to Avery as I lean against the wall. It makes me happy, a surge of pride rushing through me. The fact she was smart enough to get Addy and get the hell out of there. I can't believe she thought that quickly. She knew enough to get my daughter out of harm's way. I could kiss the fuck out of her for that. In fact, when I get out of this mess, that's the plan. That and making her stay with me. I claimed her ass, but I want more. I want her next to me, in my bed every night. I want her naked and writhing beneath me. I want everything I didn't think I'd ever want again after what happened to Jenny.

I crack my neck from side to side as I think about everything. Everything I've done, who I've hurt. I think about my time in the club and all the shit I've done for them. I think about Addy. And all the time I've missed with her. I wasn't there for her first word. I wasn't there when she started to crawl. I wasn't there when she attempted her first steps. I've missed so much of my little girl's life.

A part of me is ashamed. I should have been there. The other part of me is angry that I let Jenny's death keep me from her. Maybe Avery was right. Maybe she does need me. I don't know how that would work, but maybe I need to try and be a better father to her. I need to be around more. I need to be there for all her other firsts because I've already missed so many of them.

A door creaks open, and bright light spills through the bars blinding me. I raise my hand to block my eyes and watch as one of the bastards walks into the room.

"How much you think your life is worth to your club?" he asks. I chuckle.

"You think they'd pay you for me? You're insane," I tell him.

"Am I? I think they'd pay a pretty penny to get one of their members back. In fact, I think they'd do a lot more than that for you."

"Then you're as stupid as you look. They won't pay shit for me. I'm replaceable." Lies. I know Ty would do anything, pay anything to get me back. That's what we do. That's who we are. We're brothers till the end.

"You might think so, but I believe otherwise," he snarls at me. Then I notice what he has in his hand, and I flinch. I crouch down and shove myself against the back of the cell when he grins and steps forward. I watch as he shoves the cattle prod through the bars before it hits me. A jolt of electricity shoots through my body, and there's nothing I can do to stop it. I grit my teeth and try to bear it, but it's almost too much to handle.

"We're gonna have fun with you," he laughs, doing it once more. I groan as my body twitches and falls over. I can't keep myself up after that last one. He pulls the prod out of the cell and turns to walk away, leaving me a heap.

I feel like shit. I feel like I've been handed my ass, and in a way, I have. The door is still open when another couple of guys walk in. This time the cell is opened, and I'm kicked in the ribs. Boots collide with various parts of my body, and there's nothing I can do to stop them. Pain shoots through me as I see spots in my vision. Then I'm dragged off the floor, and something clasps around my wrists. I hear the chains hit the cell bars before I'm hoisted to my feet. I scream from the pain shooting through my wrists as the cuffs dig into my flesh. Once I'm on my feet, the chain is secured to the roof of the cell. My arms are thrust above my head.

"You piece of shit," I hiss at the men doing this. "You're all goin' to die." They just laugh, and one throws a punch to my already sore ribs. I hiss a breath as he chuckles.

"I don't think it's gonna be us that dies," he sneers at me.

"Oh, you don't think so? Once my brother's find out what you're doin', they're gonna kill every one of you."

"You and your brothers aren't in a position to make threats. Not if they want your ass back," he seethes with anger.

"That's where you fucked up. I'm replaceable. They aren't gonna give you shit," I hiss.

"Oh, I bet they will. We'll see now, won't we."

Another blow to the ribs, and I want to double over in pain. There's a lot a man like me can handle, and I'm doing my best not to show them any weakness. They'll just use that to their advantage.

"Fuck you," I wheeze as they laugh and turn to leave me hanging in the cell. I watch them go, closing the cell door behind him. Once they're out the main door, I'm thrust back into the pitch-black darkness.

I don't know how long I hang, but my legs are getting weaker. My arms are numb and painful. I wish I could just get my hands on one of those motherfuckers and make them pay.

I find myself wondering what Avery must be thinking. She's probably running as far from the club as she can get after this mess. I bet she won't even be around once I get out of this shit I'm in. If she were smart, she'd run. She'd get the hell away and never look back because all I bring is grief. I can't be what she needs. I can't be what she even wants. I claimed her for my own selfish reasons, and I can let her go just the same. But do I want to let her go? I don't think I've felt anything like I do when Avery is near me. Sometimes I'm happy to have her around, and that's unusual for me.

Then there's Addy. I make a vow here and now to be a better dad to her. She deserves that much after what happened to her mom. She deserves more than I can offer, but she doesn't deserve to be without her dad. I tell myself that I'm going to be there for her. I'm going to take care of her and love her as she deserves.

With a sigh, I need to figure out a way out of this mess first. Every second wasted in here is a second I could be with them. I close my eyes, and I can see her. Grabbing Addy and running. It was such a smart move on her part. If I could have opened my mouth and told her to do something, it would have been that, but everything happened so quickly. I watched for as long as I could before I blacked out. I don't think they went after her. At least, I didn't see them go. I'm sure they would have said something by now if they had them, which leads me to believe they don't.

I couldn't praise her enough for saving that little girl. She did the right thing. I would have lost my shit if anything happened to Addy. I'm her father, and I'm supposed to protect her from all the bad things in life. The more I think about it, the more pissed off I feel. How did I not see them coming? Was I so wrapped up in Addy and Avery that I missed the warning signs? Did they just come out of nowhere? There are too many questions I don't have answers to. But for now, I can relax. I can breathe because I know Avery got my little Addy back to safety.

CHAPTER FOURTEEN

AVERY

There's a sick feeling in the pit of my stomach. I've been nauseous all damn day. I don't know what it could be apart from the stress of everything that's happening. Addy sits on the floor on a blanket playing with her toys as my stomach churns. A knock on the door pulls my attention from her. I walk over and pull it open to see Tyrant standing there. I move to the side to allow him into the room before I walk over and sit on the floor across from Addy.

"You find out anything?"

"Not much. We're waitin' on them to make a move. They obviously want somethin'."

"Like what?"

"Our area. They want us gone."

"And you can't make that happen." He chuckles and shakes his head.

"No. I can't make that happen. This is home. This place is home to all of us."

"What about Shade?"

"It's been two days. I figure they'll be callin' with their demands soon."

"And if they don't?"

"They will. Assholes like them always do. Pine is the president over there. I know him well enough to know he wants somethin' he's just waitin' us out."

"Why would he do that?"

"To keep us guessin'. I'm sure he's torturin' Shade for information about the club." I suck in a breath at that. I can't imagine him being tortured. A tear slips down my cheek as Ty curses under his breath.

"I forget you aren't a part of this world some-times." I wipe the tear from my cheek before looking up at him.

"Would it make a difference?"

"No. It's still hard to hear. I just need you to understand that the man they took is probably not gonna be the man they return."

"What does that mean?"

"Just what I said. If the Demon's are torturin' him, he won't be the same, Avery."

"Just get him back, Tyrant."

"I'm doin' my best, darlin'. You good with the little one?" he asks, nodding toward Addy.

"We're fine."

"He's gonna need you around, you know?"

"I'm not going anywhere."

"You sure about that?"

I've thought about it over the last two days. I want whatever this thing is between Shade and me. I want to see what he has to offer. Would it be easy for me to stand up now and just walk away from all of it? Of course, it would. I could walk away and never look back, but in the back of my mind, which isn't what I want. I want more of him, and Addy is growing on me. I want her. I want us.

"I'm here, Tyrant. I don't have any plans on walking away from him."

"Even if he isn't the same man as before?"

"Even then," I state.

"I'll hold you to that. Come down in a bit. Have one of the girls keep an eye on Addy. We'll talk about this some more." I nod my head as he looks at Addy, then turns and leaves the room. I watch him go before lifting Addy into my arms.

"Your daddy is going to come back to you. You mean too much to him not to come back," I tell her as if she can understand me. She jabbers and makes noises before tugging at my hair.

"I'm not letting those girls near you either," I promise her. No one will be messing with Addy but me. I won't allow it. I highly doubt Shade would want that either.

I stand from the floor and carry Addy out the door with me. I walk back to the main room and find Tyrant and the guys sitting at a table. I walk over and take a seat when Ty looks up at me.

"Didn't I say to get one of the girls to watch her?"

"Yeah, I'm not doing that. She's my responsibility."

"Since when?"

"Since your brother claimed me, that's since when. I'm not letting one of the girls watch her!" I snap at him this time. Cowboy chuckles and shakes his head.

"My old lady can watch her, Avery. She isn't a club whore," he says. I shake my head. This is on me. I pushed him for more, and he gave it to me.

"Fine. We have an idea where they might be holdin' Shade. It's an old, abandoned police station."

"How far away is that?"

"About twenty minutes. We can hit it head-on, or we can wait on them to call."

"Fuck them calling! Go find him!"

"I thought you'd say that," Ty chuckles as the

others smile at me. What the hell are they smiling about? This isn't the time to smile.

"What is so fucking funny?"

"You are," Cowboy replies pushing my last button.

"What the hell?"

"You're just so ready to go and handle this like no other issues are standin' in our way."

"What issues?" I ask, looking between them.

"The fact that we don't know one hundred percent he's in there. Or maybe how many of them we are up against." I release a frustrated breath.

"So, what do we do?"

"I vote we wait on them to call." Tyrant suggests. I don't know how well I like the idea of waiting on the Demons to call. What if they don't call? Then what happens? What if they demand something that they're not willing to give? What if they want more? There are so many things that could go wrong with all of this. I look down at Addy as she chews on one of her toys and sigh.

"Okay."

"You're good with that?" Ty asks as I nod my head.

"She needs her dad back."

"And she'll have him back. We just need to play this the right way," he tries to reassure me.

"I'm just on edge," I admit.

"I know you are, darlin'. We all are. This isn't an ideal situation, but we'll handle it." I nod my head as Ty's phone rings. I watch him hold up a finger to all of us before answering the phone.

There's a lot of one-sided talking coming from him as we all glance at each other. Is that them? Are they making demands? I'm so on edge I can feel myself shake, but I know I need to calm down for Addy's sake. A few deep breaths, and I get myself under control as we all watch Tyrant for a reaction.

"I can do that," he says into the line. "I want proof he's alive." It has to be them. My chest clenches as I think about him. He has to be alive. What the hell does he mean he needs proof? My insides churn as I think about what he's saying. Does he think he's dead? No, they wouldn't think that way, and neither am I.

Tyrant hangs up the phone, running a hand through his hair before looking back at us.

"They have him. They want a million upfront for his return."

"A million dollars?" I gasp at the amount.

"Yeah. Shit, we shouldn't be talkin' about this in front of her," he adds, looking to the guys.

"She has a right to know," Bull says. Just as I'm about to say something, his phone pings. I watch him open it up, and then his face falls. I stand, passing Addy to Bull before taking the phone from his hand. He looks up, shocked that I just did that, but I don't care. Yet when I look down at the grainy picture on the screen, I know I shouldn't have. I shouldn't have touched that phone. My hands begin to tremble as Ty stands to his feet, wrapping his arms around me.

"He's gonna be okay."

"Did you look at this?" I scream.

"I saw it," he answers softly.

"He's ..." I can't finish that sentence. All I can see is a man who has been beaten to hell and back. The blood, the bruises, the swollen eye. Tyrant takes the phone from my hand and passes it to Cowboy as he pulls me in closer.

"He's gonna be okay."

"How can you say that? I saw him!" I cry.

"This is why I didn't want you involved, Avery. You can't handle this shit. I'm only gonna say this once, and that's it. He's gonna need you to be stronger than this. Shade's gonna need you to be able to handle him when he gets back. This isn't a game. This is life!" He roars, causing Addy to cry. I look over at the little girl on Bull's lap and know he's right. He will need me to be strong and keep a straight head because I'll need to help him with Addy. I'll need to help him recover.

I sniffle a few times before wiping at my eyes. I walk over and lift Addy into my arms, soothing her until she stops crying.

"Fine. I can handle this."

"Can you? Because right now, I'm not so sure," he snaps.

"Is he here? No, he isn't. I'll be fine once he's here."

"You sure about that?"

"I'm sure." With that said, he nods his head as the others pass the phone around, looking at what they're up against. I wish I hadn't looked at that phone. I wish I hadn't seen the broken man on the screen.

CHAPTER FIFTEEN

SHADE

All I feel is pain. They come in, beat the shit out of me, and then leave me hanging here. My legs have given out more times than I can count, but I still try and force myself to stand. The cuffs slice into my wrists as I hang here praying for something. Death maybe? I don't know how long I've been here. I don't know what the hell is going on outside of here. Did they contact, Tyrant? Does he know what the hell is happening to me? My mind is nothing but fog. I hang onto the thoughts of Addy and Avery to keep me going. Knowing they're out there waiting for me helps. Deep down, I wish I were with them. I wish I were with Addy.

The more I think about my life, the more I think I need my daughter in it. I haven't been fair to her. I haven't been fair to my parents or me.

They're good people, but they don't deserve to be stuck raising my daughter. I should be doing that. I should be the one taking care of her, and I haven't been doing that. Jenny would be so disappointed in me.

"I'm sorry," I whisper to the nothing that exists around me. "I'm so fuckin' sorry." What am I sorry for? Not taking care of my child? Not caring enough? There's a list of shit that I'm sorry for.

Then there's Avery. The woman I claimed without her even knowing. The one who calms the storm inside of me. How can I care this much about her when I only just met her? How can I know that she's something I want to keep forever? She feels like home to me, and that's not something I've felt in a very long time, if ever. I thought Jenny was it. I thought we could make something out of our lives, but she wasn't one to settle down. What if Avery isn't ready either? I didn't give her much of a choice in the matter.

Not that I care. I don't, really. I claimed her, and now she's mine. Both of the girls are mine. I want Avery around while Addy is there. I want to see that interaction between them that I saw at the park. And the fact that she kept my daughter safe? That means everything to me. More than I can express in words. She put her own life in danger for Addy. That tells me what kind of person she truly is. I can trust her with Addy.

I never asked her about being a parent, though. I don't know if she wants kids or even likes them, for that matter. Although, she did seem taken with Addy. That doesn't mean she wants to step up to the plate and take Addy on. Maybe she isn't interested in being a mother to another woman's child. The thought crossed my mind, but I shook it off and ignored it. She wants me, and I come with baggage in the form of a one-year-old little girl. She can either deal with it or walk. Except I don't want her to walk. I want to keep her. I want to have her around.

"Wake up, princess!" I hear one of the assholes enter the room. I'm barely hanging on at this point. After being beat on, I zone in and out.

"What the fuck do you want?"

"It's your lucky day. Your club decided you were worth it," he announces. My skin crawls. I hope they didn't do anything stupid. But then again, these are my people. My brothers. My family. I would do anything for them, and I know they'd do the same.

"What are you talkin' about?" I ask before I'm punched in the ribs. I wince, trying not to let him see the look on my face.

"They're comin' for you." I ignore him and watch as he walks back out of the room. What did you do,

Tyrant? What were his demands? No one has told me anything aside from what that asshole just said. It makes me wonder what the fuck they wanted from Ty.

After what seems like forever, I hear a commotion outside the room. Then the door opens and in walks the guys.

"Fuck," Cowboy hisses. "I'll get bolt cutters." He turns and walks away as Tyrant opens the cell door quickly and wraps his arms around me, lifting me.

"You been like this the whole time?"

"Pretty much." My head lolls to the side as Cowboy comes rushing in with the bolt cutters. In minutes, he cuts my arms free, and they fall in front of me. My shoulders burn, ache from being stretched the way they were. My legs about give out, and Ty lets me slide to the floor to sit.

"You can't walk out of here," he says.

"I can damn sure try," I snap at him.

"Don't fight me on this, Shade. We're carryin' you out. Doc's at the clubhouse waitin' on you."

"What did they want?" I ask, needing to know.

"A million," he replies as I curse under my breath.

"We need to move," Rain yells into the room. Tyrant grunts as he and Cowboy lean down and pull me to my feet. My legs are weak as I try to make them work to walk out of here, but it does no good. Ty grabs one leg, and Cowboy grabs the other, lifting me off the ground. They carry me out of the room, and I see the rest of the guys walking around taking things in. They all nod at me, telling me they're happy I'm alive. I don't know how I feel.

"A million isn't worth it," I tell Ty. He chuckles.

"You don't think so?"

"Hell no." my throat is dry from not having anything to drink in what feels like days.

"How long was I in there?"

"A week if they stuck you in there straight away," Rain says as he walks along next to us.

"Fuck," I grumble. A week. A week of being tortured to no end. A week of being mistreated and abused. What the hell were they thinking? That they'd get the money, and then it would all be over? They have a surprise coming when I've recovered from this shit. Once I'm healed, I'll go after them. All of them.

The door is opened to the back of the truck, and the guys lift me in as I try my best to maneuver into the seat. My body nearly falls as I try to brace my weight on my arms. I shake my head, pissed at myself for being this weak and pissed at them for making me like this.

"This is bullshit," I mumble under my breath.

"It's pretty fucked up, but you're home," Tyrant says. I nod before my head falls onto the back of the seat. I don't think I've ever been so thankful to sit down in my life.

"The girls?" I ask, needing to know they're safe.

"They're fine. Avery's been takin' care of Addy." That makes me smile, knowing she stepped up to do that. It makes my heart happy.

The ride back to the clubhouse doesn't take us long. Before I know it, I'm being helped inside. My legs barely work, but I make an effort. We get down to my room, and I know I need a shower, but I also want to see Addy and Avery.

"Where are they?" I ask as I shove off Tyrant and move toward the bathroom. My legs almost give out each step I take.

"Had them go to another room for a bit. I didn't want you to get overwhelmed." I nod my thanks before heading for the bathroom. Turning the water on, my chest tightens. What if they had killed me? What if I never got to see my daughter again? The thoughts assault me as I slowly pull my clothes off, wincing every step of the way. Then I climb in the shower on shaky legs pressing my hands to the wall trying to hold myself up. The water hits me, causing pain every step of the way. A few minutes later, the shower curtain pulls back, and a naked Avery steps in. My cock responds to her, but I ignore it because the pain is too much.

Avery reaches around me grabs the soap before squeezing it into her hand. Then I feel her hands on me. Massaging me, she works her way gently around my body, cleaning me. I step under the water to wash the soap away as she looks up at me, tears in her eyes. I just shake my head, not wanting to answer anything or talk about it. She gives me a soft smile before climbing out and grabbing two towels. She wraps herself in one before holding the other out to me. I take slow steps to climb out, holding the wall for leverage. Avery wraps the towel around my waist as I make my way back into the bedroom. I head straight for the bed and sit down, out of breath. I can't believe this is what it's all come down to. I can barely stand, and it hurts to sit. Avery moves around the room, pulling her clothes on as she goes.

"You want me to get your clothes?" she asks softly. I nod, and she moves through the room, grabbing some clothes before setting them on the bed next to me.

"I don't think I can hold Addy," I say.

"I'm right here."

"I know you are." I want to push her away. I want to tell her I don't need her help, but that would be a lie. I do need help, and I hate that feeling. I've never been one to admit defeat, yet here I am.

Avery helps me into my pants before helping me pull a shirt over my head. The pain is almost unbearable. I swallow hard before she stands and looks at me.

"Do you want to see her?"

"Yeah, I do." She nods her head and walks out of the room before coming back a few minutes later with Addy in her arms. It does something to me seeing the two of them together. It causes my chest to tighten.

"Who is that? Huh?" Avery coos at Addy as she walks toward me. Addy's eyes light up, and a smile tugs across her face as her little arms shoot out toward me. I nod for Avery to bring her closer before I try and lift her. My arms don't want to work with me. I sigh as Avery holds her on my lap. I lean down and press a kiss to the top of her head.

CHAPTER SIXTEEN

The doctor has checked him over and said that overall he's in good shape. I don't see it that way. I know when someone is telling you something just to appease you. I don't need that kind of shit. I'm a nurse, for fuck's sake. I think that's part of the reason the doctor agreed not to take him to the hospital. That and the fact that Cowboy knows what he's doing with him. I told him I'd be here. Day and night. And I will. I took a leave from work to focus just on him.

"He's glad you're here," Bull says as he rolls up next to me.

"I don't know about that. He's moody."

"Come on, nursey. You can handle a little moody, can't you?" he teases.

"I handled you just fine," I remind him with a smirk.

"That's right. And if you can handle me, you can handle Shade." I nod my head.

"It's more than just him, though. It's Addy too. He doesn't want her to go back to his parents."

"And you're not ready to be a mom." It's a statement I'm confused about. I don't mind taking care of Addy, but I don't know if I'm ready for this full-time. I have a job that I love. It feels selfish even to think that right now.

"I love my job, Bull. I love helping people."

"You're helpin' him." I blow out a breath before sitting on the stool.

"I know, I'm trying to. It's just a lot."

"Then take a break."

"I can't do that."

"Why do you need a break?" I hear his voice, and it sends a shiver down my spine. I turn to look at Shade over my shoulder where he stands. One hand braced on the wall for balance.

"I don't."

"Bull just said you did." He comes toward us and sits on the stool blowing out a breath. "You can go."

"What?"

"You can go. I don't need a babysitter anyway," he states, casually as if it's nothing.

"What the hell?"

"What? I'm just statin' a fact," he says.

"And Addy?"

"I'll manage."

"Why are you being so stubborn?" I ask him. He's acting like an ass right now. I can sense it. Shade's trying to play the calm role, but I can feel the tension in him. What is his problem?

"You need a break? Do you need a way out? I'm giving it to you, Avery. I'm lettin' you decide your fate right now because I'm too weak to fight you."

"What the hell does that even mean?" I snap at him. He sighs and raises his hand, running it through his hair.

"It means this shit isn't over. I'm goin' after those motherfuckers once I'm better. It means you have one chance to walk away from me. Just one," he says. Another chill crawls down my spine at his words. Just one chance. I should go. I should run from him and this club. I should force my legs to work right now, but they won't.

"Jesus," Bull mumbles under his breath.

"Last chance, Avery." I look at Shade and wonder what life could be like with him. Is it always this complicated and scary? Is there always going to be someone out there looking to hurt him? What if they can't get him back next time? There are so many questions I have no answers to. So many things that I'm unsure of, but the one thing I am sure of is what I feel when I'm with him.

"I'm not going anywhere," I state. Bull chuckles, but Shade just stares at me, a war in his eyes. What is he thinking right now? Did he not want me to stay?

"Don't ever think you're gettin' out of here then." I don't know why but I like the sound of that. I don't want to leave. I want to be with him and Addy.

"You're stuck now," Bull adds with a smile on his face. Shade is still serious as he grabs a bottle of water and unscrews the cap. I watch him drink, his throat bobbing with each swallow before I see one of the girls with Addy. I keep an eye on her, making sure she's taking care of her.

"You don't like the girls holdin' her?" Shade asks.

"No. I know what they're here for, and I don't think taking care of Addy is in their best interests," I tell him as I shove to my feet and walk away from them. I walk across the room, and without another word, I pull Addy from the girl's arms. She doesn't look offended, but she should be. Maybe she's good with kids; I don't care at the moment.

With Addy in my arms, I walk back over and sit on the stool once more. Addy babbles and makes noises while Shade stares a hole through me. As much as it causes heat to stir inside of me, I ignore him.

"You're good with her," Bull chimes in.

"She's easy to love," I tell him. Then I realized what I'd said. I love Addy. I love the little girl who's been attached to my hip for the last week. I've grown accustomed to having her in my arms, feeding her, caring for her. I don't think I could let this part go even if I wanted to.

"You don't mind?" Shade asks.

"Mind what?"

"That she isn't yours." Is he trying to push my buttons? Is he trying to piss me off?

"Does it matter? She needs to be taken care of, and I think I've been doing a good job of that," I snap at him. His lips curl into a smile before he laughs. I don't think this is funny. I think he's an ass because he wasn't here to take care of her, but I was. And I did. And I will continue to do so.

"Don't fuck with her, Shade. She's been the best thing for Addy this last week," Bull tells him. I give him a thankful smile before he nods back at me.

"I didn't say shit. I was only askin'.'"

"No, you're pushing for a fight. If you want me gone, just say the words, Shade. I don't need you picking at me," I tell him as Addy lays her head on my shoulder.

"You're not goin' anywhere," he growls.

"Then stop pushing."

"I was only askin' a question. Stop bein' so dramatic."

"Me? What about you?" I snap at him. His eyes move from mine to Addy and back. I know she's fallen asleep it is her nap time.

"I'm taking her to bed. You should rest too," I finally give up and tell him. I stand from the stool and walk away. Heading toward the room, I wonder if he will come rest with his daughter. She's missed him; I know she has.

When I get to the room, I enter and lay Addy on the bed before climbing on next to her. I lay with her curled up in my arms, sleeping peacefully. A few minutes later, Shade walks in and kicks off his boots. He pulls his cut down his arms, wincing before tossing it onto the chair next to the bed. Then he climbs onto the bed on the other side of Addy and lays down facing her.

"You're good with her. I can see that," he says.

"But?"

"But she isn't yours, and I didn't know if that bothered you."

"It doesn't. She needs love, and that's all I've done." He nods his head before slipping his hand past Addy and laying it on my hip. Slowly I watch his eyes flutter closed and his breathing even out. He finally falls asleep as I watch the two of them. Addy rolls over and cuddles into his chest, his hand coming down to wrap around her. My chest swells with happiness for them. They are their own little family.

It makes me wonder what it would be like to stay with both of them. What would life look like for us? Even though I don't know much about Shade, I know enough. I know I want to be with him. I know I want both of them in my life.

With a sigh, I scoot closer and pull the blankets over all of us and finally fall asleep peacefully for a change.

CHAPTER SEVENTEEN

SHADE

Waking up to both of them the other day did something to me. Even though Addy had a crib in the room, having them both in my arms was perfect. I've never felt as content as I did that morning. I slept through the night peacefully without any bad dreams. It was nice. And something I want more of.

"I'm goin' after them," I tell Tyrant. He nods his head.

"When you're better," he agrees.

"I am better. It's been a week."

"You're not healed yet, brother. Give yourself some time. Those motherfuckers aren't goin' anywhere."

"What if they do?"

"They're not. They got the money, and now they're out blowin' it. New bikes and shit. I've got eyes on them," he explains, and I shake my head. That isn't enough. They're buying bikes on our club's money. The thought pisses me off, but I know there's nothing I can do about it right now. If Ty says no, the answer is no.

"I want them bad, Ty."

"I know you do. And you'll have them," Ty promises before bringing his beer to his lips. I watch him take it down before setting the bottle back on the counter in front of him.

"I'm gettin' better," I tell him.

"I know you are. But you're not a hundred percent yet, and we aren't movin' until you are. We don't need any other setbacks."

"But you agree we go after them?"

"Fuck yeah, I agree. Look what they did to you!" He snaps, and I know he's telling the truth. We'll get them back.

"Heard that."

"You look better," Cowboy comments as he takes the seat next to me.

"I feel better. Still sore and shit," I admit.

"That'll heal up. How's shit with Avery?"

"Why? What happened?"

"Nothin'. Just askin' is all. She hasn't left yet," he reminds me. I know she hasn't, and she isn't going to.

"And?"

"And I was wonderin' why."

"Because I said no, that's why."

"Damn, you're moody," he grumbles, grabbing a beer of his own.

"You're too damn nosey," I tell him. Just then, she walks into the room with Addy on her hip. Avery's eyes find mine, and damn, I can see my future in those. I can see so much more with that woman than I ever thought possible.

"What's that look?"

"I think I love that girl."

"You think?" Ty asks.

"Yeah, I think. I don't fuckin' know what that feels like."

"Yeah, you do. You loved Jenny once," he says, and I know he's right.

"This is more. What I feel is more," I tell him, and it is. I don't know how it happened so damn quickly or what the hell I'm doing, but I feel it.

"Then you need to stop bein' a dick," he tells me.

"I'm always a dick."

"I know that, but you don't need to be, not to her."

"She likes it," I chuckle. The guys shake their heads before Avery walks over and sits.

"She's hungry again," she tells me. I nod my head and motion for her to pass me Addy. She does, and I hold my daughter in my arms, kissing the top of her head. Avery stands and leaves us alone, going to make her something to eat.

"You hungry?" I ask Addy as she looks around at the guys. She smiles like she knows she belongs here.

"She's so damn cute," Cowboy says.

"She looks a lot like you, brother," Ty adds.

"I know. It's weird some days seein' just how much she looks like me."

"Would you change it? If you could?"

"Which parts?"

"Jenny."

"No. I wouldn't have Addy. I would change leavin' her with my parents, though. It took them beatin' the hell out of me for me to realize just what I needed to do. She needs me."

"I think you're right," I hear Avery before she sits on the seat next to me once more. I see she has a little plate of food in her hand, and I turn Addy around so she's facing her. Avery scoops some food onto the spoon and puts it in her mouth as I watch in awe of her. I haven't fed her yet. Since I've been back, Avery has done everything for her.

"Can I?" I ask, nodding toward the plate. A huge smile breaks out across Avery's face as she nods her head and passes me the spoon. She takes Addy from me and sits her on her lap before nodding for me to go ahead. I scoop the food onto the spoon and bring it to her lips just as she blows a bubble. The food goes everywhere but in her mouth as everyone at the table laughs.

"You not hungry now?" I ask her scooping up some more. This time I actually get it into her mouth.

"I gotta piss," Cowboy mumbles before standing and walking away. Ty moves to do the same, and then it's just the three of us.

"You okay?" Avery asks me.

"I'm good. I was just thinkin' that I need to spend more time with her. She needs more of me," I admit to her.

"I think she'd love that."

"What about you? I want more time with you too."

"I'd love that, Shade. I just want you to get better," she says softly.

"I am. One day at a time, baby."

"Good. Addy needs you," she says.

"What do you need?" I know what she needs. I don't need to ask, but I do anyway. She needs me, and that's that. She needs everything I'm willing to give her.

"I just need you to get better."

"I am, but what else do you need?" she doesn't answer, and I smirk at her. "You need my thick cock fillin' you? You need to feel me burst inside of you?" I ask her. Her cheeks turn pink as she looks up at me under her lashes. It's fucking perfect. This woman is fucking perfect.

"You shouldn't talk like that in front of her. One day she's going to learn those words," she says with a grin on her face. She likes it when I talk to her like this. I know she does.

"Not yet. So tell me. You want my cock, Avery?"

"I want all of you, Shade." That hits something deep inside of me. Something I thought was long since buried after Jenny. I wasn't sure I was ready for feelings and emotions, but sitting here with just the three of us, I like it.

"Let's get her a nap," I tell Avery. She shakes her head like I've lost my mind, but I'm tired of waiting. I've waited a week for her pussy to be wrapped around me. I've waited for her, and now I'm going to take her.

CHAPTER EIGHTEEN

We walk back to the room with a sippy cup of milk and Addy in tow. Shade lays her in the crib with her cup, and she happily drinks it, her little eyes fluttering closed. I knew she was getting tired and needed a nap.

Shade doesn't waste any time moving in on me. His hands are wrapped around my waist, tugging me against him when his lips come down on my neck. I shudder and suck in a breath as he sucks my flesh into his warm mouth. His lips skate over my skin as he kisses his way up my neck to behind my ear.

"You sure you should be doing this?" I ask him. I know he's healing, and I'm glad for that. I also know that he isn't a hundred percent either.

"I need this."

"I need you too," I whisper before he spins me in

his arms and kisses me roughly. I can feel my lips bruising from this kiss, and I can't help but love it. My hands wrap around his neck, tugging him closer to me. He growls low in his throat and deepens the kiss. His hands come to the hem of my shirt, and he pulls back just enough to get it off me before he's right back attacking me. My insides flutter as his fingers slide along my skin, causing bumps to form in their wake.

"You like me touchin' you?" he asks huskily as he walks me backward toward the bed. I nod my head before he slowly lowers me. Then he's pulling his cut off and laying it on the chair before tugging his shirt over his head. I watch how his muscles ripple with each movement, knowing that I can touch them, taste them and love them whenever I want. The thought should scare me, but it doesn't.

Shade pulls his jeans off and then his boxers before stepping back toward the bed. Jerking my pants down my legs, he tosses them to the side with the rest of our clothes before climbing on the bed between my legs.

"We gotta be quiet," he warns softly before leaning down and pressing a kiss to my stomach. I squirm beneath him, and he smiles against me.

"Then don't make me scream," I tell him. He looks at me and grins.

"I don't know how not to make you scream," he says. And he's probably right. Shade situates himself between my legs and grabs his cock in his hand before pressing it against me. I shift, trying to take him inside of me as he chuckles.

"You want this cock?" he asks, and I nod my head. "Show me how much. Touch your pussy," he demands. My hand slides over my thigh and between my legs, touching myself. Shade watches me intently like this is the most fascinating thing he's seen. He strokes his cock as he keeps his eyes on my hand.

"Fuck, that's hot," he hisses before he reaches up and slaps my hand away. Then his cock sinks inside of me, filling me as I bite my lip and try not to cry out in pleasure. He thrusts and hits me as deeply as he can before pulling out and starting all over. I bite my lip so hard I can taste blood on my tongue, but he doesn't stop. The slap of our skin is the only sound in the room. I reach up, wrapping my hands around his arms as he fucks me harder and harder. My nails dig into his flesh, and he lets out low grunts as he takes me.

Soon I can feel the burn inside of me. I can feel him swell, and I know he's as close as I am. Shade moves his hand between us and finds my swollen clit, circling it slowly. Pleasure shakes my body as I tremble and fall apart for him. I come hard, having a hard time keeping my cries under control. I want to scream his name. I want to scream anything, but I know Addy is sleeping, and I can't do that. Instead, I cling to him, riding our pleasure like a roller coaster until we both come down.

Shade pulls out of me and lays on the bed next to me before slipping his arm under my head and pulling me toward him.

"Fuck, that felt so good," he mumbles before pressing a kiss to my forehead.

"I've missed that," I admit to him.

"Me too, darlin'."

"I need to go back to work, Shade."

"You're my nurse."

"I mean it. I have to work," I tell him.

"No, you don't. I got you."

"That's not the point. I have patients that rely on me."

"That prick in the chair?" he asks, and I can feel the tension in him.

"Lance? No. I don't work for him anymore," I tell him. "Are you jealous?" I ask, looking up at his beautiful face.

"Goddamn right, I am. You're mine, Avery."

"I know that."

"Then don't ask me if I'm fuckin' jealous. Of course, I'm jealous. I'm a fuckin' jealous man."

"Of what?"

"Anyone lookin' at you. Anyone comin' near what belongs to me."

"Do you hear yourself? I'm not a toy, Shade," I remind him.

"Never said you were, but you are mine, and those are the thoughts that run through my head," he tells me.

"You have no reason to think like that."

"Does that mean you agree? You're mine."

"I don't think I have a choice, do I?" I tease. He smirks at me and shakes his head.

"Not really. I claimed your ass."

"I know."

"And you fuckin' like it," he adds. I do like it. I don't want to admit that to him and have him get all caveman on me, but I do like it.

"What happens now?"

"We wait. We wait until I'm a hundred percent, and then we go after them."

"Are you sure that's smart? You have Addy now."

"And I'll have her after that too."

"You know what I mean," I tell him.

"I know you worry, Avery, and you don't have to. Everything is gonna be fine."

"What if you're hurt again?" I ask softly, praying to god that nothing else happens to him. I don't know if I could take that.

"I'm gonna be fine. Nothin' is gonna happen to me. I promise."

"You can't promise me that."

"Yeah, I can. You have to trust me, Avery. You don't have a choice here," he states. He's right. I don't have a choice here. He's the only thing I care about besides that little girl. Everything hits me at once, thoughts of losing him, of Addy losing him.

Tears bite the back of my eyes as Shade looks at me intently.

"What are you thinkin'?"

"Nothing."

"Don't lie to me."

"I'm just scared, Shade. Scared for her."

"She isn't losin' me, and neither are you."

"I don't care what you say. You can't make promises like that." He sighs heavily before he shifts to look at me.

"I know that, but everything's gonna be fine, Avery. You need to calm down."

"What if you're hurt again?"

"Then we deal with it." I huff and sit up, climbing out of bed before glancing at Addy. She's still sleeping peacefully, unaware of what's going on around her.

I grab my clothes and pull them back on as Shade sits up in the bed watching me.

"What is this?"

"This is me being confused, Shade. This is me worried about you, about her. About us."

"There's nothin' to worry about."

"You keep saying that, and there's everything to worry about! You getting hurt or worse! That baby needs you," I tell him, trying to be strong, my voice betraying me.

"And I'm here, Avery. What the hell is wrong with you?"

"You know what? I need to go. I need to clear my head."

"You aren't goin' anywhere," he says firmly. I shove my feet into my shoes and head for the door, grabbing my cell and purse on the way.

"I have to. I need to think about all of this."

"There ain't nothin' to think about, Avery!"

"Don't raise your voice," I tell him, glancing over at Addy and then back to him.

"Then don't walk out that door."

"I need this, Shade. I need to think."

"Then go in the other room, but you aren't leavin' here."

"Yes, I am. I need to get back to my life too. I have work, a home that I haven't been to in a week."

"You don't need a home. You belong here." This is all too much. I feel like my head is spinning, and the fact that I want to be here with them so badly is weighing heavily on me. I don't know that I can handle him being hurt again. I don't know that I can take it.

Without another word, I turn on my heel and pull the door open just as he roars my name. Addy begins to cry, and a piece of my heart breaks from walking away from her. But I do it anyway. I walk out of the room and down the hallway. I walk through the main room catching stares as I go, and keep going until I reach my car. Then I climb in and let the waterworks go.

CHAPTER NINETEEN

SHADE

Avery walked out on me. She left. I couldn't believe it, but she did it. I told her she wasn't going anywhere, and she left anyway. How could she do that? How could she just leave? Addy needs her. I need her. She's fucking stubborn as hell, and I knew that, but I thought I made myself clear on where we stand. She's mine.

"So they have been all over Washington." I eye Tyrant as he talks. I don't know how I feel about any of this anymore. She fucking left me, and that stings.

"Buyin' new bikes and even set up a new club-house. Looks like the little fuckers are thinkin' about stickin' around," he adds. I chuckle under my breath. No, they won't be around for long.

"That's bullshit. Settin' up shop on our money," I growl.

"Seems that way. The money doesn't mean shit as long as you're back," he adds.

"That money means more now that I'm back," I tell him.

"The point is, we know where they are now. We know that the Demons have some sort of stability and plan on settlin' right here in our area. That changes things. It changes how we approach them and how we handle things. The cops are in our pockets, not theirs."

"Meanin' what?" Mav asks.

"Meanin' we use that to our advantage. I say we start small and fuck with them. We work our way up the food chain. Take out some of their prospects first," Ty lays out his plan. I nod my head. I don't mind that idea at all. Get them inside the jail with a few of our guys, and they'll regret being a part of that club.

"I'm good with that," I announce, seeing the shock in Tyrant's eyes. He wasn't sure I was going to agree to it. I know I've been hell-bent on going straight at them, but now I have Addy to think about. I know I need to play this cool and keep my head in the game.

"You are?" he asks.

"Hell yeah. When are we doin' this?"

"I've been watchin' them. Listenin'. They have a

run tomorrow night that we can stop. Tip-off our boys in blue and let them work their magic," Cowboy suggests. I nod my head. I like that idea.

"I say we go for it," Maverick chimes in.

"Me too."

"We don't need to vote on this. We just run it." Ty informs us.

"What else you got?" I ask, seeing the look in his eye. I know there's more.

"I want them all. Not only for what they did to you but what they did to Bull. I hate sittin' back and waitin' just as much as you do. I hate that we can't just go over there and blow the fuck out of them, but that would cause too many red flags even with the cops in our pockets. This is the best I can come up with right now."

"And it works, Prez. No need to worry about that," I tell him.

"You're the main one I'm worried about. Bull wants revenge, but he's limited on what he can do. You, on the other hand, are fully capable. I just need to know that your head is on straight."

"It is. I'm ready to handle this however you see fit. As long as it gets done, that's all I care about."

"And it'll get done. I promise that much. We just need to time it right," he says. I nod my head agreeing with him.

"Then that's what we do."

"Next thing. Do you think we need eyes on Avery?" he asks. Just hearing her name sends a chill down my spine. I should go after her, spank her ass for this shit, but I understand, and I'm willing to give her the space she needs. For a while anyway.

"I don't think so. They don't have anything on her."

"You sure? She's been around here a lot."

"I'm sure they just think she's here for Bull. I doubt they'd think anything else." The guys all nod their heads, agreeing with me. Not that I don't worry about her, I do. I want her safe just as much as anyone else, but I don't think they think anything of her.

"Okay. If that changes, we get the prospects on her," Ty says, and I nod my head before bringing my beer to my lips. I take a long pull before looking around the table. I can't believe I could have lost all this, that I could have lost the guys and myself.

"If that's it, then we're good here," Ty slams the gavel down on the table. We all stand, and I head out into the main room finding the girls all playing with Addy. I know Avery didn't like it very much, but now that she isn't here, I don't really have much choice. Seeing how they are Cowboy's and Mav's old ladies, I think it's fine. There are only a few of the club girls over there playing with her. I know the girls will watch out for her.

"She's happy," Mav says, slapping a hand on my shoulder.

"I never knew how much I was missin' out on, brother. I knew I was missin' shit, but damn. I missed her first-time crawlin', her first tooth. Mom said she was tryin' to take a step not long before I got her."

"That's a hard one, brother. But she's here now. You have her now. You won't miss anything else."

"But is she safe here? We do all kinds of fucked up shit, Mav. I don't want her involved in that shit," I tell him truthfully.

"Then get a place. Have one of the girls go watch her while you're here." That makes sense. I nod my head thinking about that. It's a good idea. I've been thinking about finding a place of my own lately.

"I might do that. In fact, I'm gonna look some up now," I tell him, pulling my phone out of my pocket. I click on the internet tab and start browsing when I hear Addy cry. My head snaps up immediately, finding her with my eyes. Then I stalk toward her and hold out my arms.

"You miss daddy?" I ask her. She comes straight to me and snuggles into my arms. Damn, I missed this too. I missed bonding with her, just being with her. "You're okay," I soothe her.

"You're good with her," Beth, one of the club girls, tells me.

"Thanks. She's pretty easy to deal with." She smiles before walking away, and I carry Addy down the hall to the bedroom. I sit on the bed, keeping her in my arms as I search through my phone. Finding a few places I wouldn't mind looking at, and I take a screenshot to check into them more after Addy goes to bed for the night.

I lay her down on the bed and grab a diaper and her pajamas off the nightstand.

"You ready to get some sleep?" I ask her as she chews on her hands. She grins up at me, and it's the best feeling in the world. I pull her shirt over her head and wonder if this is the right thing to do. Keeping her here, with me. When Avery was here, I felt so sure. Now, I doubt my ability to take care of her on my own. I haven't had to. Avery was here helping me with her.

I pull her little jeans off and change her diaper before sliding her feet into her pajamas. Then I move to her arms, sliding them in before zipping them up.

"You're the cutest little thing," I tell her as she smiles at me.

CHAPTER TWENTY

AVERY

It felt good to get back to work. It's been a week since I've seen Shade or Addy. I miss them both, but I need some time to decide if this is what I want. Do I want to step into the role of mother? Am I ready for that? I don't know that living in the clubhouse is the best option for Addy either, but how do I tell Shade that? They could move in here. They could live with me. I have three bedrooms no one uses.

"Jesus, Avery. Listen to yourself," I mumble as I throw my legs over the edge of the bed and climb out. It's Saturday, and I don't have any patients today. The thought of going and seeing Addy has been sitting heavily on my mind. I should stay away and think, but the more time I spend away from her, the more I miss her. I want her in my arms. I want Shade in my arms.

I head to the closet and pull out some clothes before dressing. After brushing my hair and making myself look presentable, I head out the door, grabbing my keys. When I walk to my car, I notice a bike sitting down the street. I squint my eyes, trying to see if it's Shade or not. No, that's not him. I brush it off and climb in my car, pulling out of the driveway. Driving right past the person, they don't even look my way as I pass. I pull out onto the main road and head toward the clubhouse. The drive doesn't take me long, and the thought of seeing Addy makes me happy. A smile tugs across my face as I pull into the parking lot and climb out.

"Hey, Avery," Maverick says as he strolls toward me.

"Hey. Shade here?"

"He's inside."

"Thanks. Oh hey, you guys don't happen to know someone in my neighborhood, do you?" I rattle off the address as Maverick thinks about it.

"Not that I know of. Why?"

"I just saw a guy on a bike over there. I've never seen him before," I tell him before turning and heading inside. I walk in, and I can feel the air shift around me. This feels like home. This feels like exactly where I need to be.

"Nursey, you came back. Did you miss me?" Bull asks as he wheels toward me.

"Hardly. You look good, though. Following my directions?" I ask him.

"As much as I can."

"Good. Shade around?"

"I think he was puttin' Addy down for a nap." He nods toward the back. I nod and walk through the room and down toward the bedrooms when I hear him humming softly. I push the door open slowly and see him standing with her in his arms. She looks so tiny compared to him. I watch the way he sways slightly, rocking her to sleep. Then I watch as he lays her down in her crib, pulling a blanket over her. A smile tugs across my face just as he turns and sees me standing here. He looks back at Addy once more before coming toward me and closing the door behind him.

"She just fell asleep. She's been a little cranky today."

"I missed her. I ..."

"I get it, Avery. It's a lot to deal with."

"It's just ... I'm so confused, Shade. I want this, I want you and Addy, but I need to be sure. I wouldn't want to be in her life and then just disappear. That goes both ways. You need to be sure, too," I tell him. He grabs my hand in his and leads me toward the main room before sitting me at a table and sitting across from me.

"If I weren't sure, I wouldn't have claimed you, Avery."

"You barely know anything about me," I remind him.

"I know enough. I know that when shit gets, bad you step up to the plate. I know that you can handle things you never thought you could," he says. It makes my heart swell that he knows that about me.

"But are you sure about all of this? Being together? Me stepping in with Addy?"

"Listen, I've blamed myself over the years. I still do for what happened to her mom. Would I want someone else to take her place? No, I wouldn't, but she isn't here anymore, Avery. She's gone, and there's nothin' I can do to change that. I want you. I want you here."

"About that part. I don't like the thought of Addy always being here. She needs a home, a safe place to be."

"I'm lookin' at a few houses later today."

"What? You are?"

"Yeah. I agree. She needs stability."

"You agree? With me?" I ask, a little shocked he said that. Shade chuckles and nods his head.

"Yeah. I do."

"Why don't you move in with me?" I blurt out. I thought about it but brushed it off as being crazy, but if we're going to do this, why not? It would give Addy stability, and we wouldn't be far from the clubhouse.

"Move in with you?"

"Yeah. I have two extra bedrooms no one uses. You wouldn't have to look at any houses. It's minutes from the clubhouse," I tell him, although I sound like I'm rambling. Maybe I am rambling. I'm nervous and with good reason.

"You think that'd work?" he asks me.

"Why wouldn't it? She would have a room, or she could sleep in our room and have a playroom. Whatever works better," I tell him. He stands from his chair, and I think he hates the idea of what I just said, but then he's pulling me to my feet and kissing me like I'm the air he needs to breathe.

"What are you doin' to me, Avery?"

"I don't know. The same thing you're doing to me?"

"What am I doin' to you?"

"You're making me feel things I didn't think I'd ever feel."

"Then I guess that makes two of us."

"So, what do you think?"

"I think I'd love that, but don't think Addy won't be spendin' time here. These are her people, her family. They will protect her with their lives if it comes down to it."

"I know that. I think I'm figuring that out."

"Good. I want your input on things. I want your help with her," he admits, and my heart soars.

"Thank you."

"You took care of her when I couldn't. You were there for her when I wasn't able to be. That means more to me than you'll ever know." His words are sweet and kind, and that's the opposite of how he normally is. He's typically grumpy and bossy, but this side of him is something I've never seen before. I raise my hand and rest it on his cheek before smiling.

"Are you going soft on me?" He bursts into laughter before looking down at me.

"Not a chance in hell. In fact, you've got an ass-whoopin' comin' your way when that baby wakes up."

"I don't think so."

"Oh, I do. I specifically remember tellin' you that you weren't leavin', and you did it anyway. That deserves punishment."

"You wouldn't do it," I tell him before he laughs once more.

"You don't think so?"

"Nope. I don't."

In seconds, he has me spun around, facing away

from him before his hand collides with my ass. A few guys look over, hearing the smack as my cheeks heat. I'm about to stand up straight when he lands another one.

"Don't make me keep this up, Avery. You're not goin' anywhere ever again," Shade tells me.

"Jesus, Shade! Everyone can see you!"

"That's the point, darlin'. Then you won't think about doin' it again."

"I wasn't thinking about it," I tell him.

"And now you won't in the future," he grins at me.

"So you think moving in with me is a good idea?"

"I like it, darlin'. I think Addy would love it too."

"I'm going to check on her," I tell him. He nods his head as I walk away and head down the hallway. Opening the door, I step inside and see her sleeping peacefully. I just needed to see her.

I walk over and lean down, pressing a kiss to her forehead before tucking her in a little tighter.

"She likes you too," I hear his voice behind me. I turn my head just as Shade walks over and wraps his arms around me. This is perfect. This is what I want.

CHAPTER TWENTY-ONE

SHADE

"Prospects are in jail as of this mornin'." Ty sits at the head of the table and delivers his update.

"Thank fuck."

"Yeah, Wiley isn't too happy. He's losin' his shit as we speak," Cowboy chimes in.

"I bet he is," I say as I smirk at the guys. This is good news. Pine is the prez over there with the Demons.

"We got guys on the inside fuckin' them up a little. I told them not to go too hard," he laughs.

"Yeah, I bet you did," Mav says, making us all laugh.

"I think our next move is to take a few members down."

"Down or out?" I ask, needing clarification. If I had my say, we would be taking them out.

"Whatever you wanna do. I honestly don't care either way," he answers casually.

"Then I say we take them out," I tell him.

"I don't care either way as long as they aren't fuckin' with us any longer."

"Grab one and let's see what we can get out of him," Ty suggests. The guys all nod their agreement before church is called to an end. I walk out of the room and spot Avery in the corner with Addy in her arms. They're both smiling and happy, and it makes me happy to see. I never thought I'd find someone like her. I never thought I'd want another woman, not after what happened to Jenny. I still carry the guilt, the hate around in my heart. I still feel the pain as if it happened yesterday.

"You okay?" Maverick asks, stepping up next to me.

"I'm good. Just thinkin' about everything," I admit to him.

"About her?" he asks, nodding toward Avery.

"Yeah. She asked if I wanted to move in with her."

"No, she didn't."

"Yes, she did."

"Who the hell in their right mind wants to live with your moody ass?" he asks, causing me to chuckle a little. I know I can be over the top at times, but that's just me.

"Apparently her," I tell him.

"You gonna do it?"

"Why not? I was lookin' for a place anyway, right?"

"Heard that. It might be a good thing for Addy. But what are you gonna do with her while Avery works?"

"I don't know yet. Daycare? I hate the fuckin' sound of that shit, though."

"I don't blame you. I don't know that I'd want my kid in daycare either. What about one of the girls watchin' her?"

"Girls are always here. Avery thinks she needs some time away from the clubhouse to adjust to a home," I tell him.

"What do you think?"

"I don't know, brother. Maybe she's right. She's used to livin' with my parents, and then I tossed her into this mess. Maybe she needs to be at home."

"I think, either way, she's a part of this club, Shade. She's gonna have all her uncles around her regardless of where she's at."

"I know. That's what I want too. I want her to grow up and have all this. I want her to feel the love we all have for each other."

"You're her dad. You know what's best for her, but I think a break would be good for her," he tells me. I nod my head before grabbing the beer one of the girls sat in front of us. I take a long pull as I watch Avery talking to Mav's old lady. It makes me happy she gets along with all of them too. I didn't need that worry on my shoulders.

"She's a good girl," he adds.

"Yeah. She really is." She turns at that moment, our eyes connecting. And right this second, I know it. I'd do anything for that girl. I would sacrifice myself for her. The feeling hits me harder than I'd expected it to. I didn't expect to ever find this either.

I motion for her to come to me, and she does. She walks across the room, a smile on her perfect face. I reach for Addy and take her passing her off to Maverick before pulling Avery into my lap.

"What are you doing?"

"Whatever the fuck I want," I tell her. She shifts in my lap, and my cock responds. I don't know how any straight man can be around her and not get a hard-on.

"In front of everyone?"

"You think I'd let them see what belongs to me?" I growl before kissing her neck. "Not a chance in hell."

"We need to talk," she says softly.

"I know we do. There's a lot that's about to change, and we need to figure shit out," I tell her.

"I want to quit my job," she blurts out. I chuckle and kiss her neck once more.

"Done."

"What? What do you mean? You're not mad?"

"No. I was gonna suggest that anyway. I know you didn't want any of the girls watchin' Addy."

"That's what I was thinking too. And I don't want her in daycare," she says, making my chest swell with pride.

"We're on the same page then."

"We are? I mean, I know I need to cover my half of the bills and all. And I will; I have some saved. I just think it's smarter this way," she rambles as I suck her flesh into my mouth and moan.

"I got us covered, baby. You don't need to worry about anything," I tell her.

"I have to help, Shade."

"You wanna take care of Addy?" I pull back and ask her seriously.

"Yes, I do."

"Then you do that, and I'll handle the rest. It's easy."

"Is it? That easy?"

"It is. You take care of her, and I'll take care of you." My lips are back on her flesh as she sighs like that was the biggest relief in the world, and maybe it was to her. I like that she's thinking about Addy that way. That she's worried over her safety and who's going to be watching her. It just shows me how much she cares, and I love that.

"Are you going to keep this up long?" she asks me as I run my tongue along her shoulder.

"As long as I feel like it," I tell her before I continue. She squirms in my lap, and I have to grab her hips in my hands to stop her from moving. I don't think my cock can take much more of that.

"When do you want to move?"

"I don't own much. We can move Addy's stuff whenever you want."

"Then why aren't we doing that now?"

"You sure you're ready for all this?" I ask her once more.

"I wouldn't have brought it up if I wasn't ready, Shade."

"Okay, darlin'. Let's go move some shit," I tell Avery, standing her to her feet and slapping her ass.

CHAPTER TWENTY-TWO

The guys have been working hard moving all Addy's things from the clubhouse to my house. They also went and picked up whatever was at Shade's parent's house. They were sad to see her go after having her so long, but I think they were also happy that he's stepping up to the plate and taking on his responsibilities.

Now I adjust things in the room to the way I want them. I hang little pictures that I bought on the wall of princesses and little furry animals. I thought she might like them.

"It looks good," Mav says as he stands in the middle of the room with Addy in his arms. She takes it all in, glancing around as if she knows this is her new room. She couldn't possibly, but it still makes my heart melt seeing her in here.

"Thanks. Did they finish getting everything?"

"You got it all. Shade is unloadin' his shit, but there isn't much besides clothes."

"Okay."

"You sure about this? Them movin' in? More so him movin' in?" I turn to face Maverick and lean against the crib.

"Yeah, why? Should I be worried?"

"No. He's just a moody bastard."

"I think I can handle him," I tell him with a grin. Addy reaches for me at that moment, and I walk over, taking her from Mav.

"She's attached to you."

"She's a good girl. Aren't you, Addy?" I ask her, watching the way her face lights up. She's the most perfect little thing I've ever seen in my life. I see the way Addy's little eyes are slowly falling closed and look at the clock on her dresser. It's time for her nap. I lay her down in her crib, kiss her cheek, and cover her up before walking toward the door with Mav right behind me. Closing it softly, I know she'll fall asleep almost instantly.

"You're good with her," he says.

"Thanks. I'm trying." He nods his head as we both walk out into the living room. I step outside when I hear the rumble of bikes coming our way.

The guys stop what they're doing and look down the road just as the bikes come into view.

"What the fuck?" Mav mumbles under his breath. We both step out onto the porch as the bikes pull to a stop. The guys pull their guns, but they're outnumbered. There's more of them. There's only Mav, Cowboy, and Shade here. My heart starts beating a little faster.

"Well, I'd say this is a nice change," the man declares as he climbs off his bike. Shade turns his head to look at me, a silent warning in his eyes. I start to back up to go back inside when the man spots me. His gun comes up, aiming at me.

"Don't move," he growls as I stop in my place. My heart beats erratically in my chest as I look between him and Shade. Addy is inside asleep. What do I do?

"What the hell do you want, Pine?" Shade asks when he's had enough.

"You know, I thought about that all the way here. What I wanted. At first, I just wanted to bend that pretty little bitch over and show her a good time, but then you were here," he replies, making my skin crawl. He was coming after me? In my own house? The thought causes my stomach to roll.

"You touch her, and I'll kill you," Shade warns calmly.

"Once I got here and realized you fuckers were here, it sort of ruined the plan. You took one of ours, and you got my prospects locked up and beaten."

"I don't remember doin' any of that." Shade has a smirk on his face.

"Then let me remind you," he snarls before motioning for his men to move. Guns are aimed as they advance on the guys. My heart beats faster, knowing I need to get to Addy. I step back, but the main guy, Pine, they called him, steps up the porch and in front of me. He presses his gun against my throat and slowly brushes my hair away from my shoulder with it.

"Leave her alone!" Shade roars.

"Fuck you!" the man in front of me screams but never takes his eyes off me.

"You're a pretty little thing." The smell of alcohol is heavy on his breath. I try not to cringe, not to piss him off any further than he already is.

"Get away from me," I tell him, trying to keep as calm as I can.

"Oh darlin', I think I'm gonna keep you." My skin crawls as I glance toward Shade. A man is standing next to him with a gun pressed against the side of his head. Tears burn the back of my eyes as I blink them away.

"Stay the fuck away from her!" Shade yells as the

other guys laugh. This isn't going to end well. I can feel it. Something inside of me stirs, and I feel sick to my stomach. The man in front of me grabs my wrist and pulls me off the porch. Shade roars before the guy next to him slams the butt of the gun into his head. Shade immediately falls to the floor as I scream for him.

"Shade!"

"You would think you assholes would learn not to fuck with us the first time. Or hell, the second, for that matter," the man snarls as he clings to my wrist. I try to pull away from him, but his grip is too tight.

"Let me go!" I snap at him, but he just chuckles.

"I don't think so. When they return what they have of mine, I'll return your ass in the same condition." He spoke loud enough that they all heard him.

"Done. Let her go, and we'll release your guy," Maverick says.

"I doubt they'd be in the same condition then, would they?" he smirks at him. I swallow hard, trying not to throw up all over the asshole, but the feeling is there.

"Don't hurt her," Maverick says once more.

"I'll do what I want with her. You have twenty-four hours to return my guy." With that, I'm dragged toward a van. I look at Shade as he shoves to his knees, his eyes stormy. The guy next to him hits him once more, and I see his eyes roll back before he hits the ground.

"No!" I cry out before I'm thrust into the back of the van. I shift around and sit on my ass before scooting against the side of the van. It doesn't take long for it to take off, throwing me around like a ragdoll.

CHAPTER TWENTY-THREE

SHADE

I finally came to, and she was gone. I wanted to believe it was all just a bad fucking dream, but it wasn't. Mav and Cowboy's old ladies are keeping Addy while we have prospects on the house. They all have shoot-to-kill orders if anyone comes back. The thought of leaving them there didn't sit easily with me, but Addy was asleep. I didn't want to disturb her.

"We need to move on this. They have Avery," I repeat as Tyrant eyes me.

"You think I'd let them take your old lady and not move on this?"

"Then let's fuckin' do it."

"I put the call out, Shade. The bastard is playin' games now," he adds. I know he is. He's hurting her. I can feel it. I can feel it in my bones. He's pissed at us for what we did, and now he's taking it out on her. When I get my hands on that motherfucker, he's going to wish he'd never laid a hand on her. Pent-up anger simmers inside of me, and when I unleash it, hell is going to break loose.

"This is bullshit," I mumble as I run my hand through my hair.

"It is. I can't believe they showed up at your place, brother."

"Me either. Just pulled the fuck up. They'd been watchin' her," I say.

"They must have been to know where she lived."

"This is all fucked up," Cowboy sighs before lighting up a cigarette. I reach over and grab myself one, lighting up alongside him.

"We could just raid their clubhouse," Mav suggests.

"We could. Or we could wait for him to call us back."

"Neither sounds like a good option. The longer we wait, the more they hurt her."

"But stormin' the place doesn't make sense either. She could be hurt in the process. We don't know if that's where they have her to begin with."

"That's true too," Cowboy mumbles.

"This is all so fucked up!" I roar, slamming my hands down on the table. I'm pissed. I'm beyond pissed. They put their hands on her. They're more than likely hurting her as we speak, and there is nothing I can do. Not a goddamn thing. We storm their place, and she might not even be there.

"Let's go talk to the little fucker," I say. Ty nods his head, not really caring what I do at this point. We all shove out of our chairs and head for the door, one right after the other.

We head outside and straight to the shed where we're holding the asshole and step inside.

"Where the hell would they take a hostage?" I ask, first thing out of my mouth. He looks up through his swollen eye and grins.

"You'd like to know."

"You better answer him," Ty warns before picking up a screwdriver. The guy just laughs a sick dark laugh but doesn't answer. Ty walks closer, slamming the screwdriver into his shoulder before pulling it free. The man howls in pain as I ask again.

"Where the hell would they take them?" I ask once more. I can feel the rage simmering inside of me. The thought of killing the asshole is strong, but as Pine said, he'll return Avery in the same condition, and I can't have her dying on me. I can't have that on my shoulders too. I need her too much. Addy needs her.

"Fuck you," he groans as Ty slams the screwdriver into the other shoulder. He screams louder this time, and I smile. Fucking prick. He's stupid for not giving me what I want. He's not as smart as I thought he would be.

"Last chance, asshole," I tell him as Ty positions the screwdriver at his temple. All it would take is one thrust, and he'd have it planted in his brain.

"Fuck! The clubhouse! They'd take them to the clubhouse. We don't have shit else set up yet," he cries out. Ty lowers his weapon before setting it on the table next to him. I want nothing more than to stab it through his heart, but I can't, and I know that. If I want Avery back, I can't risk this asshole's life.

"What we do here, Ty?" I ask him needing him to tell me right now. Because with the mood I'm in, I'm ready to roll. I'm ready for blood, and I don't care at this point whose it is either.

"You wanna take the chance to hit their club-house? She could get hurt," he reminds me.

"She's already gettin' hurt! You think he isn't torturin' her right now?" The asshole in the chair laughs again before I step up and punch him in the face. Then his laughter stops.

"This could end badly," Tyrant states. I know it could. I know that, but I need to get my girl back. I scrub my hand over my face taking a deep breath and letting it out before I look at Ty once more.

"I can't stand to think about what they're doin' to her," I tell him. He nods his head. He has to understand that.

"I know, brother. But stormin' it and not followin' his rules is gonna piss him off even more. You ready to risk that?" Fuck no, I'm not. If we don't make the trade, he might kill her. Fuck! This is so messed up. I was standing there. And there was nothing I could have done. We were outnumbered and outgunned. This is a complete fucking mess.

"Fuck!" I roar before slamming my fist into the asshole's face once more. Maverick pulls me back and shoves me toward the door, where I gladly go. I need the air. I step outside and inhale deeply before cracking my neck from side to side.

"She's gonna be okay," Cowboy says.

"You sure about that?"

"I'm pretty damn sure. If she can put up with your ass, she can handle anything." His laughter echoes in the night, and I find myself laughing along with him. He's right, though. She deals with a lot of shit from me.

"She's a strong one," I say.

"No shit. She agreed to be your old lady and let you live with her. Not even I would have offered that shit," he adds, making me smile.

"Heard that."

"He has twelve more hours. That's it," Ty announces as he walks out of the shed. I turn to face him now, seeing the angry look in his eyes.

"He say anything else?"

"No. Just that they would have her at the clubhouse," he says.

"And we're not goin' in."

"I think it's best to wait this one out, Shade. He may pull the trigger early if we do that," he tells me. He's right. I know he is, but that doesn't stop the feeling in my chest. That doesn't ease the ache of knowing they have her. I need her here. Addy needs her here.

"Then we wait it out."

CHAPTER TWENTY-FOUR

I've never been so sick in my life. I bend over and throw up once more, but I've done it so many times nothing is coming out. I'm just thanking God that I'm not vomiting blood at this point. They've beaten me, kicked the shit out of me, and I can almost guess I have some kind of internal injury. My stomach cramps as I hold onto it, begging this to be over.

After what seems like forever, someone comes into the room and drags me to my feet. I don't know who the hell he is, and I don't really care. I stand and limp my way out of the room with him leading the way.

"It's your lucky day!" Pine, the piece of shit, declares as I make it into the main room of their clubhouse.

"Why is that?" I manage to ask.

"Your boyfriend decided to trade for you after all." I could kiss Shade and kill him at the same time. I saw him get pissed and go after that guy only to get hit again. He should never have done that. He's still healing from what they did to him before. Anger sits heavily in my chest, but what can I do? It's all done and over with now.

I limp my way down the hall and into the main room, where I see some guys. Blood trickles down my thighs as I take a deep breath, knowing exactly what that is. I don't want to face reality. I don't want to tell Shade, but as Tyrant's eyes clash with mine and slowly travel over my body, his fists clench. It isn't what he's thinking. They didn't rape me, thank god. But they did beat me. My left eye is swollen and sore, and my lip is busted and crusted over.

"I offered a fair trade," Pine says as I look at the condition the other guy is in. It's not even close to fair. They beat the hell out of that guy, and now he barely stands on his own.

"Seems fair to me," he says, nodding toward me. Pine turns and eyes me up and down before shoving me in his direction. I stumble and nearly fall but manage to right myself when Maverick steps forward and shoves their guy toward them. Everything else happens in a blur. The sounds, the feelings. All of it. Maverick grabs me and shoves me behind him before

I hear the shots being fired. The door is kicked open and more guys come storming in. I've never seen so many guys since I've been at the clubhouse, and it makes me wonder where they all came from, but I don't have time for questions. Maverick moves us through the room and out the door before rushing me to a truck. I'm thrust into the backseat before he slams the door, slapping a hand on the top, letting them know to drive. I wonder where Shade is. I didn't see him in there.

I keep quiet as the prospect drives us toward the clubhouse. I don't utter a word even though my heart is breaking and my body is battered.

When we pull in, I see him waiting outside the front doors, Addy in his arms. My sweet Addy. I want so much to hold her, kiss her, and let her know I'm here. When the truck comes to a stop, the prospect comes around to help me out, and I'm thankful for that. My legs are wobbly as I step down, and he wraps his arm around me.

"Lean on me," he says as he walks us around the truck. Shade comes into view, and his eyes drop down, covering my whole body before I see his nostrils flare. He passes Addy off to Bull as I shake my head.

"I need to hold her," I murmur as we get closer. He nods and lifts her back up, and walks toward me slowly. He doesn't know what to say or how to react to this. Frankly, neither do I.

"Here," he says when he's standing in front of me. I use all the strength I have left in me to hold her in my arms. I kiss her head, her cheeks and just cuddle her to my chest. She doesn't cry or make a sound as I hold her to me. I kiss her a few more times before passing her to Bull. Then Shade is there. Pulling me into his arms and holding me just like I need.

"I'm sorry. I should have done more," he says.

"You didn't have a choice. I'm okay."

"Did they ..."

"I think I'm having a miscarriage, Shade." The words hurt, leaving my lips, and a sob escapes. He pulls me in tighter and keeps me there, kissing the side of my head. My heart sits heavily in my chest as he leads me inside.

"The doctor is here," he says as he walks us through the main room and back toward his bedroom. I want to cry. I want to scream, but I don't do either. I let him lead me.

"I need to shower," I tell him.

"Let him check you first," he says.

"No. I want to shower, Shade." He nods his head, and I walk away from him, heading into the bathroom. I flip on the warm water and peel out of my dirty, blood-stained clothes, discarding them on the floor at my feet. Then I step in and let the tears fall. They mix with the water and slide down my cheeks. Shade doesn't get in, and I'm grateful that he knew I needed some time. I wash and climb out, finding a fresh set of clothes sitting on the counter waiting for me. I dry and quickly dress before walking back into the room. The doctor, I assume, is standing there silently while Shade sits on the bed with his head in his hands. He must hear me because he lifts his head, his shaggy hair tumbling into his eyes. He looks so damn perfect sitting there like that. My chest clenches as I walk to the bed and sit next to him.

"Would you like him to leave?" the doctor asks. I nod my head. I don't want him to be here when he tells me the baby is gone. The baby I didn't even know was growing inside of me. Something breaks in my chest, and I know it will never be whole again. Shade stands and turns to me, pressing a kiss to the top of my head before leaving the room. I'm sure this was hard for him too.

I lie back on the bed and let the doctor do his thing. It shocks me when he pulls out a Doppler and squeezes some gel onto my stomach.

"I'm pretty sure I miscarried. There was a lot of blood," I tell him even though it breaks my heart.

"Let's be sure," he says, pressing it to my stomach. My inside clench as he moves it around. Tears burn my eyes, but I try to blink them away. He keeps moving it over my stomach until I hear it.

"There we are. It was hiding from me," he says with a smile. How can this be? How did I not miscarry?

"I don't understand," I say softly.

"There may have been trauma, but the baby sounds good. Possibly some breakthrough bleeding. I can't be sure at this point, Avery. I need to see you in the office," he says.

"Of course. But ..."

"But for now, the baby has a great, strong heartbeat." My chest inflates. The baby is okay. I'm still pregnant. Elation surges through me. Happiness burns the back of my eyes this time. I don't know if this is what Shade wants, but the baby is okay. That's what truly matters here.

"Oh my god," I cry as I cover my face with my hands. The doctor finished checking me over to tell me I have bumps and bruises that would heal. I already knew that. He also said I should rest as much as I can until I can get an appointment in the office. I agree and watch as he leaves the room and Shade walks in. He walks over and sits on the edge of the bed, holding my hand in his.

"You're gonna be okay."

"Did they get them all?"

"Pine is still alive. He's mine," he says in a low growl. I nod my head. I understand that.

"I'm ..."

"What? You're what?"

"I'm pregnant," I tell him. His eyes light up, although he doesn't smile. He licks his lips and nods his head.

"Not like I did much to prevent it."

"Are you mad? I know you have Addy." His hand comes to rest on my stomach, a strange look in his eyes.

"I always wanted a big family. That was something my mom couldn't have. She tried to, but it just didn't happen. Are you ready for this?" His stormy eyes come to meet mine, and I can see the rest of my life reflected at me. I can see all the love, all the emotions.

"I am. I love Addy," I tell him.

"I love you, Avery."

"You do?"

"Yeah, I do. I don't want anyone else. Just you," he says, causing me to melt under his gaze.

"I love you too."

"And we're havin' a baby. I can't wait to tell the guys." He smiles at me.

"I'm scared. What if what they did hurt it?"

"Not a chance. That baby is mine. It's strong like his mom and dad. There's no way anything hurt it," he says surely.

"What about Addy?"

"What about her?"

"That's two kids pretty close in age, Shade."

"It won't be bad. There's two of us."

"I really do love you. Will you lay with me?"

"I'd do anything for you."

CHAPTER TWENTY-FIVE

SHADE

I had to leave her. I didn't want to, but I had to. I have to finish what the guys started. They didn't let me tag along for that shit because they knew I'd lose myself and kill everyone in sight. Ty was right about that. I would have. I would have killed them all and not thought about it, but they're all dead now anyway. All except Pine, and he's hanging on by a thread. I walk toward the shed with the guys all behind me. They know what this is, know how this ends, and they have my back.

Pulling the door open, I step inside, the light filtering in around me as I do. Pine lifts his head barely to register that I'm here.

"Fuck you," he growls as I smirk at him.

"You almost took two things from me, asshole. You almost took my child and my woman."

"The fuckin' cunt was pregnant?" he asks with a grin on his face.

"Still is. Seems you failed at both attempts, right?"

"Had I known, I would have made damn sure neither of them left my clubhouse."

"The one that burned to the ground?" I see the way his eyes twitch. He didn't know we blew that fucker sky high. No, I wanted to be the one to tell him that.

"You didn't."

"We did. And now it's time you pay for what you did." I grab the knife off the table and walk toward him as he watches me. I don't give a fuck about him. I don't care about dragging this out anymore. I just want him dead. I want it all over with so Avery can relax and move on with her life. With our lives.

I press the tip of the knife against the side of his eye before pressing it in. He screams as I carve the fucking thing out of his head. He looked at my girl. He watched her lie there and bleed, and for that, he loses this first.

"How you feelin', Pine?" I ask as the mother-fucker passes out from the pain. I don't give him a chance to lie here. I slap his face until he wakes back up, and then I press the knife against his throat. I drag it straight across, listening to him gag and sputter. Then I step back and take in my work. He's bleeding out as he pulls at the binds holding his arms in place.

"You're not leavin' here alive, you son of a bitch," I spit at him. He gasps and gags a little more before the life slowly seeps out of him. I watch his eyes as all the life leaves them. I watch him struggle to take his last breath, and I don't even feel bad about it.

"She okay?" Cowboy asks.

"She's pregnant," I tell them all.

"No shit?" Mav is shocked.

"No shit."

"Damn, Shade. Two babies?" Tyrant chuckles.

"Not bad, right?" I turn to look at them.

"Not bad at all. You happy about that?"

"I would have waited till Addy was a little older, but I think we got this," I tell them as I grab a rag and wipe my hands.

"I think so too," Tyrant adds as we all turn and walk out of the shed.

"I need your help."

"For what?"

"I got a project I'm workin' on for Bull. You in?"

"We're always in, brother," Cowboy says, causing me to smile. I know I got the best fucking friends I could ever ask for right here with me. I know they'd do anything for my girls or me.

"What is it?"

"It's a goddamn surprise, but I need to see my girls first," I tell them. Mav laughs as we all walk back inside. I spot Avery on the couch in the corner laying down with Addy not far away. She keeps her head tilted to the side so that she can see her, and it makes my chest fill with pride. It hasn't been easy. I didn't think it would be, but I've seen how Avery has taken over the role of mother to Addy. I don't know if she fully sees it or not. I don't know if she realizes she's doing it, but I can see it, and I'm thankful every second of the day I have her in my life.

"How's our nurse?" Bull asks when he wheels over and stops next to me.

"She's a fighter," I tell him. He passes me a beer which I gladly take and bring it to my lips.

"She's a feisty one," he says.

"She's gonna be fine. Just needs to heal up," I tell him before sitting in the chair next to me.

"What else?"

"What do you mean?" I ask him.

"I see the look in your eyes. What am I missin'?"

"She's pregnant."

"No shit?" I glance over and nod my head at him. His lips curl into a smile as he looks at me.

"You got our nurse pregnant."

"She isn't your nurse anymore. She quit her job," I tell him.

"What?"

"You heard me. She quit to take care of Addy."

"And you're okay with that?"

"She's the one who brought it up, brother."

"Damn. She's a good nurse too," he says, shaking his head.

"She is, but she wanted this. I wouldn't force this on her; you know that."

"I know. I just didn't see her steppin' away from somethin' she loved so much."

"She loves Addy more. I never thought I'd find someone that accepted both of us, Bull."

"But you did." I nod my head.

"I did. And I don't regret a fuckin' second of it."

"You shouldn't."

"I do regret what happened to you," I admit to him.

"We've been over this. It wasn't your fault. I made the choice to go out that night," he says, ignoring me.

"Doesn't change the facts. I put in for you to go."

"You're right. It doesn't change the facts, Shade. I'm still here, yeah? Just a little different than before. The only thing I regret is that I'll never ride again." I see the hurt in his eyes, and I hate it. I fucking hate it.

I nod my head and bring my beer to my lips before glancing over at Avery. She laughs loudly, the entire room lighting up from her laughter. The girls all laugh with her, and Addy smiles happily down at her from the other girl's arms. It's perfect. It's my perfect.

CHAPTER TWENTY-SIX

AVERY

I hold Addy on my side as we watch Shade work. My bump is getting bigger every day, and Addy is growing too. I love being her mom. I love being with her and everything about her.

"Okay, explain this to me again," I tell Shade. He stands from the ground and glares at me with that angry look in his eyes that he gets. I almost laugh.

"When will you listen?" Yes, he's still as moody as he used to be.

"When you explain it better," I tease him. He steps around the motorcycle and motions to what he made.

"This was an old sidecar. I reinvented it. These little ramps will let Bull wheel up onto that platform. Those hooks right there will secure his chair to the platform so he can ride again."

"You came up with this yourself?"

"Yeah. It killed me when Bull said he regretted not bein' able to ride again. I hated the look in his eyes. It pissed me off and filled me with guilt."

"It wasn't your fault," I remind him.

"Doesn't change the facts, Avery. Stop tryin' to make it better. Anyway, now he can ride," he says, looking at what he made. It's a smart idea, and it makes sense. Bull will surely be happy and surprised by this.

"I think you're amazing."

"I think you are. You're walkin' around with our daughter in your arms carryin' another inside of you. That's amazin', darlin'."

"When are you going to show him?" He walks away from the bike and comes straight toward me, pulling me into his arms. He roughly kisses me as Addy slaps at him. Then he turns and presses a kiss to her cheek before she laughs.

"Dada," she says softly, and we're both surprised. Addy has been a little slow at talking, but the doctor didn't seem concerned. She mumbles but never has said a word until now.

"Did she just say that?" he asks.

"She did. She said, dada," I coo at her.

"Say it again, darlin'. Say dada."

"Dada," she says once more. The smile on

Shade's face couldn't possibly get any bigger. It lights up the whole outside.

"You love your dada?" he asks her before kissing her cheek once more. Addy laughs and leaps into his arms before he turns back to me.

"What about you? You love your daddy?"

"Oh, I'm calling you daddy now?"

"I wouldn't mind it when I got you bent over the bed screamin' my name. Or when I'm face first between those thighs eatin' the best meal I've ever had," he says, causing me to blush. I love that he can get that reaction out of me. Not many have been able to, but Shade always does.

"You shouldn't talk like that in front of her. She's learning words now," I tell him.

"She doesn't know what I'm talkin' about yet. Tell me, Avery. Do you like when I eat your pussy like it's my last meal? Like I'm a dyin' man on death row?" My body responds to his dirty words just like it always does. My insides tremble as he steps closer, grabbing my pussy in his hand. I want to grind against it, feel him touching me, but we're standing outside, and Addy is right here.

"You're playing a dangerous game, Shade."

"You've been so fuckin' horny since you been pregnant. I want your pussy on my face tonight. I want you ridin' my tongue until you can't come anymore. You hear me?"

"I hear you," I reply breathlessly.

"Do you want that? You want me to eat your pussy?" he asks me.

"Yes."

"You want my cock buried inside of you?"

"Yes."

"What are you two doin'? Makin' more babies?" I hear Bull speak. I giggle and kiss Shade once before he passes Addy back to me.

"Glad you dropped into our moment, asshole."

"You shouldn't be fuckin' outside anyway. Any pervert in a wheelchair could be watchin'," he adds with a laugh.

"Speakin' of wheelchairs. I got something for you," Shade tells him. I watch him spin around and walk over to the bike, showing Bull what he made.

"The fuck is that thing?"

"This is for you to ride again, brother," Shade tells him. Bull looks at it funny before Shade walks over and grabs the handles of his wheelchair. He shoves him up the small ramps and onto the platform before securing the chair.

Then he walks around and climbs on the bike, revving it.

"You tried this out before?" Bull asks. Shade looks over, a smirk on his face.

"Fuck no."

"You're gonna kill me. I can feel it," Bull tells him as I laugh. "Stop laughin' nursey! You're gonna be in charge of my recovery!"

"Like hell she is. You're gonna be fine."

"This don't feel safe, Shade."

"Nothin' we do is safe, asshole. Shut up and enjoy the ride," Shade tells Bull while motioning for me to come to him. I walk over, and he grabs my hip, jerking me into him before kissing me roughly.

"I love you."

"I love you too."

"I'll be back. Let me take this fucker for a ride," he tells me. I nod my head and step back, watching him pull out with his cousin attached to the side. Bull raises his arms in the air as Shade takes off.

"Fuck me!" You can hear Bull yell. Addy and I stand back and watch as Shade rides him around the parking lot.

That's when it hits me hard. This is my life now. This is my family, and I wouldn't change that for the world.